A Distinguished Thug Stole My Heart

Meesha

Lock Down Publications and Ca$h Presents

A Distinguished Thug Stole My Heart
A Novel by *Meesha*

Meesha

Lock Down Publications
P.O. Box 1482
Pine Lake, Ga 30072-1482

Lock Down Publications
Like our page on Facebook: Lock Down Publications
@
www.facebook.com/lockdownpublications.ldp
Cover design and layout by: **Dynasty Cover Me**
Book interior design by: **Shawn Walker**
Edited by: **Tisha Andrews**

Stay Connected with Us!

Text **LOCKDOWN** to 22828 to stay up-to-date with new releases, sneak peaks, contests and more...

Thank you!

Submission Guideline.

Submit the first three chapters of your completed manuscript to ldpsubmissions@gmail.com, subject line: Your book's title. The manuscript must be in a .doc file and sent as an attachment. Document should be in Times New Roman, double spaced and in size 12 font. Also, provide your synopsis and full contact information. If sending multiple submissions, they must each be in a separate email.

Have a story but no way to send it electronically? You can still submit to LDP/Ca$h Presents. Send in the first three chapters, written or typed, of your completed manuscript to:

LDP: Submissions Dept
Po Box 1482
Pine Lake, Ga 30072

DO NOT send original manuscript. Must be a duplicate.

Provide your synopsis and a cover letter containing your full contact information.

Thanks for considering LDP and Ca$h Presents.

Acknowledgments

This book is dedicated to my Granny! I love and miss you so much, Ladybug. This ones for you!

First of all, I would like to thank the man that took the chance on my craft. Cash, I appreciate you in so many ways that I don't know where to begin. You are a great mentor and I took everything you said to me in stride. I wouldn't be excited about writing as I am now without your encouragement. Thank you for everything, BOSS-MAN!

My biggest supporters throughout this book were my mom and my Lil Big Bro! Thank y'all for sitting up listening to me read to you guys. LOL. The two of you don't know how that made me feel to know that I have y'all backing me one hundred percent. I love y'all to the moon and back.

Tameka, Pam, Monique, Drina, Krystal, Gigi, Katrina and Monica Skye. Thank you guys for the encouraging words and the motivation that you guys gave me throughout this time. You guys made me see that my work was great, even when I didn't see it. I appreciate y'all so much. You ladies are AWESOME!

Destiny Skai...Thank you so much for the countless hours of listening to me stress and for all of the great pointers you shared with me. I appreciate you more than you know.

To my Soldiers in the Meesha's Soldiers Group, thank you guys for rockin' with ya girl and giving a new author a chance.

Love u all,
MEESHA

Meesha

Chapter 1
Three months earlier
Sabrina

"This shit is for the muthafuckin' birds, bestie! How the fuck do this nigga think what he's doing is ok? I've sat back and let his ass disrespect me over and over and hadn't said a damn word, but not tonight! I'm tired. He's gonna learn today that he has fucked up my good girl image. This ain't me! I don't talk like this at all and you know this shyt!" I screamed into the phone.

I was sitting in my livingroom venting to my best friend, Ziva, about my foolish ass fiancé, Kelvin. This nigga had taken my kindness for weakness for the last fuckin' time. I mean this shit didn't just start happening and I'd always fell for the bullshit ass explanations he threw back at me. Nope not anymore. I'm done with this shit. I got bitches playing on my phone, putting up posts on social media talking about "this bae"! What the fuck!

"Sabrina! I'm gonna need you to calm the fuck down! I'm always here when you want to vent about that no good muthafucka, but I'm not the one to tell you what you should do. If you end this shit, so be it. But if not, I'm still gonna be here for you. All I'm waiting on is for you to say go because I'm gonna be on his ass like white on rice, fuckin' him up! You already know, if you rockin', I'm rollin'!" Ziva exclaimed.

"I hear you, Z."

"This shit ain't new. I'm not saying that you shouldn't be hurt. You have every right to be. I'm just as mad as you are and he ain't even my nigga! You are all I give a fuck about, but *you* need to decide when enough is enough. Can't nobody make that decision for you. It's all yours, baby girl." Ziva preached.

Everything she said was the truth. My mama always said that the truth hurts and Ziva had been my friend for a very long time. She would throw shade sometimes, but she had been right by my side. She spoke her mind no matter what and didn't care what anyone thought about it.

"Well, thanks for listening to me vent, bestie," I said as the front door opened.

"I'll call you back. This nigga just walked in," I whispered.

"Who the fuck you on the phone with, Sabrina?" Kelvin barked, walking into the living room. He was looking good, but I was done. It wasn't the time to be lusting over his ass. I wanted to kill him at that point.

I stood up from the couch with my eyebrows raised. "Who do you think you're talking to, Kelvin? You must think you're talking to one of them busted up hoes that you be fuckin' with? Don't come in here beating your chest like you runnin' shit around here," I screamed, rolling my eyes.

Kelvin stood there looking at me with his head cocked to the side. "Nah, baby. I know what house I'm in. My shit! So, if you want to continue to have a place to stay, I'll advise you to check your tone. I don't know where the fuck you learned to disrespect a nigga, but make that yo' first and last time, ma, for real," he said harshly, walking further into the room.

But that didn't deter me from getting shit off my chest. He had never put his hands on me, but that night I knew he just might because I went in on his ass.

"That's cute, boo," I chuckled. "How the fuck is you gonna threaten to put me out of my shit? Yeah, I knew when you walked in this muthafucka talking greasy, you came to the wrong bitch house."

I had allowed him to move in my house with me, how he opened his mouth to say that this was his place was beyond me. I paid the bills here, not him. Even though he worked as an X-Ray technichian at the University of Illinois on the south side, he barely gave me money for anything. I had to ask him for whatever I wanted from him.

Walking towards him, I stared his ass right in the eyes. I was tired of being that timid bitch that allowed him to walk over me. It was time to show him that I'd been through too much with his ass to settle.

"See, you failed to realize that I'm the bitch that held your ass down when you didn't have nothing! I dressed your ass, I bought you a car, I gave you a place to rest your head, I paid your muthafuckin phone bill! Nigga, I'm the one that provided every, muthafuckin', thing, you, needed when you got with me, I said clapping my hands. You didn't choose me! I chose your ass! The way it's lookin' now, I chose wrong." I was grilling his ass so hard I felt the heat coming out of my pores.

He stood there with his mouth hung open in shock. His eyes were bucked and he was speechless. "Babe, what's wrong with you?" he finally asked. His demeanor softened and he walked over to me trying to wrap his arms around me.

Pushing him off and shaking my head, I threw back, "Nope, Kelvin. That's not gonna work up in here tonight. You are the only one that has the answers to the questions in my mind. There will be no sweet talking today. Save it for someone that's willing to listen because that's not me." See, he had never seen this side of me. Shit to be honest, I never seen it either. But I knew one thing, I was beyond tired.

"I'm gonna need to know why you continue to let these hoes get access to my number. I don't want to know how because it's obvious. You had to have been fuckin' for them to get to the phone, so that's a given. What, you don't know how to lock the muthafucka up when you leave the house? But you've mastered it whenever you're laid up with me," I said with my arms folded waiting on what smooth shit was going to come from his mouth.

"I don't know what you're talking about, Sabrina. If somebody is calling your phone, it don't have shit to do with me," he said with a straight face. He walked to the kitchen and grabbed a bottled water from the fridge. He turned and looked at me nonchalantly as if he didn't care.

Shaking my head, I made the decision to not even go through with the theatrics. *This man is a habitual liar and will continue to be*, I thought to myself. I turned and walked to my bedroom, straight to the closet. I snatched clothes from hangers, throwing his shit into a bag. He must go tonight.

I packed the bag to capacity and zipped it up. Walking out of the bedroom, I saw him standing in the hall leaning against the wall. "I think you need to take this bag and move around for a week or two. I can't deal with this shit right now. When you're ready to be a man, that's when you come back and holla at me. Until then, I'm good on you," I said holding the bag out for him to take it and get the fuck on.

But it didn't happen the way I thought it would. I guess I wasn't the only one showing another side. His face balled up so tight and turned a shade darker. If looks could kill, I'd be dead. The concerned guy was gone and in came the devil himself.

"Bitch, you think you doin' something by telling me to leave? I was just waiting on the right opportunity to let yo' gullible ass know that I moved the fuck on a long time ago." He walked up to me with his finger pointed in my face. I took a step back, but still stood my ground.

"I just didn't want yo' ass to be feeling some type of way, ready to slit yo' fuckin' wrist and shit. I kept coming to this muthafucka for you! I've been ready to leave your weak ass.

What type of bitch just gon' let a nigga do whatever the fuck he wants? A weak bitch, that's who."

This nigga had a lot of shit to get off his chest I see. I'm glad he was getting all this out tonight. Now there wouldn't be any guessing on my part about how he was really feeling. He didn't have to put on a front to stay with me. His ass had been cheating for the longest time. I kept forgiving him, letting him come back everytime. He was kind of like my security when my parents died and for me, he was all I had. But I'm not about to deal with this shit anymore. That night was the last straw. I received picture messages from his phone of him having unprotected sex with some bitch. Not only did I receive pictures, but there was a forty-five second video, as well. I couldn't see who the woman was, but I could see him clear as day.

"For me?" I asked with my left eyebrow raised high as hell. I was shocked he let those words fall from his mouth.

"Nigga, I ain't never needed you for a damn thing. Since you want to be technical, how the fuck did you get the job you have right now? Exactly, me nigga! You wasn't shit until I made you into something, muthafucka! You wouldn't be shit if it wasn't for me. You may as well say that I'm the man in this so-called relationship because I was the one taking care of you! Not the other way around! The sad part about it is you didn't have a problem with it. But the jokes on me because I allowed the shit. But guess what, homie? The gig is up. Take your ass wherever the fuck you're gonna go because here is not where you're gonna be. It's a wrap, Kelvin. I'm done! The only thing you brought to this whatever it is, is lots of pain."

I attempted to walk away from the bullshit, but before I could pivot, this nigga had me off my feet suspended in the air by my throat. He banged my back against the wall, knocking my favorite picture of President Obama and Michelle off the wall.

"Bitch, don't ever twist yo' muthafuckin' dick suckin' lips to disrespect me like that! I'll kill yo' muthafuckin' ass, Sabrina!" I tried to pry his hands from around my neck, but it was no use. His grip was tight and he had no plans of letting go.

"I should beat the fuck out of you, but that's not how I was raised. You have one more time to call yo'self disrespecting me and I'm gonna kill yo' ass. For the record, I say when shit ends between us, not you! You ain't shit without me, bitch! But I'm gonna let yo' stupid ass think about how you just popped off tonight." He dropped me to the floor and walked down the hall towards the door, grabbing his bag of clothes along the way.

"Fuck you, too, nigga. Your threats don't mean shit to me. You want to talk about disrespect, let's talk. You have been disrespecting me for the longest time and I overlooked it all. There have been so many bitches in this relationship with us, that you couldn't put your all into me." I said, pointing to myself.

"I got a couple of messages tonight that couldn't be overlooked, so I'm making the choice to leave you the fuck alone. I may not have any family in this city, but I'm never alone. You put your muthafuckin' hands on me for the first and only time. Don't let it happen again." I was looking up at him, with my hand in his face.

"You said your peace and I said mine, so there's nothing else left to be said. Get the fuck out, go back to the bitch you were fucking on. You smell just like her ass." I said, rubbing my neck.

"You a tough cookie ass bitch tonight, huh? I don't give a fuck what was said in a text. That shit don't mean nothing to me. Now you know firsthand that I was out fuckin'. Yo' ass don't have to try to figure it out. You can give me my mutha-fuckin' ring back tho', bitch! What? You thought you was gonna keep that shit? Nah, ya not!" he said through gritted teeth.

I looked down at the princess cut diamond that sparkled on my finger. I thought about how much I would get if I pawned it.

"Bruh, if you don't get yo' ass out of my house with that fuck shit," I laughed.

"Oh, you think this shit is a game, huh? Do I look like a fuckin' kid to you?

The anger emerged even more after that bullshit.

"All the bitches you stood there and called me, putting your hands on me, then gloating about fuckin' another bitch, and now you asking me for some shit that's rightfully mine? My money paid for this ring, so I'll be damned if I give it back! All the shit I put up with because of you! Dude, again, you ain't getting shit! Get the fuck out, Kelvin! And that's the last time I'm gonna say it. I'll get your ass locked the fuck up tonight, nigga," I yelled, walking towards the front of the house to the door. *This nigga is about to get the fuck up out of here.*

Before the thought could escape my mouth, I heard him coming up behind me.

"I'm about to shut yo' mouth, bitch!" He grabbed me by my shoulders and punched me so hard in my face, I fell into the door and couldn't move. All I could see was stars dancing in front of my eyes and my jaw hurt like hell. I bit the inside of my jaw and the blood on my tongue was salty. My hand instantly went to my face, but I refused to let this nigga break me.

He grabbed me by the front of my shirt and slapped the taste out of my mouth. After he slapped me, he started punching me in the back of my head over and over. Once he saw I wasn't crying as I tried to protect my head, he kicked me in the back of my leg so hard, I buckled.

"I told yo' muthafuckin' ass that yo' mouth would get ya fucked up, but I guess you thought I was playing. Pacifying yo' ass all these years had you thinking I was some type of bitch nigga, huh?"

I guess he thought I was about to answer his ass after that ass whooping he just laid on me. I didn't have shit to say. I just wanted him to leave. My silence pissed him off, so he snatched me up by my hair and started choking me.

"That was a question, bitch, and I was waiting for an answer!" he said, choking and shaking me at the same time.

If I didn't know any better, I'd think I was about to die from Shaken Baby Syndrome. I couldn't answer this nigga if I wanted to since he had cut my air supply the fuck off. I was going in and out of consciousness, but that didn't stop him. This muthafucka was losing it. A few minutes later, he finally let me go and I slid down the wall, trying to get as much air into my lungs as possible.

"I'm gon' leave bitch, but it ain't over. When I call yo' ass, you better answer. You will always be my bitch and that pussy is forever mine. Don't get no bright ideas because you will get fucked up!"

He kicked me in my side and shoved me with his foot before opening the door. He looked me in my eyes and I swore I saw the devil in his eyes.

"I'll kill yo' ass with no hesitations. Don't play with me." With that, he took my house key off the key ring, laid it on the table by the door and left, slamming the door behind him.

I couldn't move a muscle after what he'd done to me. I laid there and reflected on the relationship I had with him. I realized at that moment that I didn't really need him. I just didn't want to be alone at the time. I'm twenty-eight-years-old, a pediatrician and I'm very pretty, but he stopped complimenting me years ago. I stand 5'5", one hundred and sixty pounds, thick in all the right places, with long curly hair, so I knew that I wasn't lacking at all in the looks department.

When my parents were killed in a car accident two years ago, my girls were all the family I had left. But he was there, along with all his bull crap to keep my mind off what was going on around me. The man in my life is no more, *how did I end up loving a man that never loved me in return?*

***

I met Kelvin one day four years ago at a basketball tournament at Seward Park. Ziva and I attended these games because she always had to be seen. I, on the other hand, loved the game. We were sitting on the lower bleacher when this guy walked up.

"Hey, Z. What's up? I haven't seen you in a minute."

He was talking to her but looking at me. I acted like I was engulfed in the game and let them have their moment.

"I'm good. Where have you been stranger?" Ziva *said, standing up giving him a hug.*

The way she hugged him, you can tell that they have known each other for awhile.

"I've been around. Just had to be lowkey for a minute you know how that goes. I came out for this tournament, you know I couldn't pass up hoopin'. Who is your friend? Introduce me" He asked licking his lips.

"Kelvin, this is Sabrina. Sabrina, Kelvin," she said, rolling her eyes.

I sized him up. He had on black basketball shorts that showed all that the good Lord blessed him with, and he was shirtless. He had a Pisces tat on his chest and plenty more other oarts of his upper body. Tattoos on a man was so sexy to me.

"Hello, nice to meet you," I said, tuning back to the game.

"No, it's a pleasure to meet you, Miss Sabrina," he said, grabbing my hand. We talked for a very long time.

I learned that he was in between jobs, had two brothers, a sister, and he loved his mama. I told him that I was a twenty-four-year-old pediatrician that worked at Ingall's Hospital in Lansing, IL. I was an only child and my parents spoiled me. I lived in the north suburbs and spent most of my time working and catching up with my girls. After chatting, we exchanged numbers and promised to get together soon. When it was his time to play, I watched his every move.

"I see he has your attention, huh?" Ziva said, eating her ice cream. While Kelvin and I was talking, she had got up and walked away.

"Yeah, he seems like a nice guy. What's his backstory, Z?" I asked, lookimg over at her once he left.

"I know him from around the way. I don't know too much about him, but I'm quite sure you won't have to wait too long to find out everything there is to know about him. I'm ready to go, let's get out of here. I got some moves to make." She then got up and headed to the parking lot.

That was the day I met who I thought was gonna be the man in my life forever, but he turned out to be the man that would hurt me worse than anyone in my life.

Chapter 2
Nova

It had been months since I'd seen or talked to Kelvin. After the incident at my home, I had to take time off from work because he had fractured my jaw. I had to have my jaws wired together for damn near two months. That shit was painful as hell but I pulled through. Kelvin and I had been together for four years and he had never put his hands on me, but I knew that I deserved better than what he was offering. That's why all his calls went unanswered and so did all the frequent pop ups at my home. The relationship that we had was far from love, I settled and was pissed because so much time was invested in that so-called relationship. Never again though. The next man had to come correct.

Right now, I wasn't sweating the small shit. It was about Nova from that point on. I changed my name during that time in my life. I am now Nova Charmaine LaCour. I hated the way my name rolled off Kelvin's tongue, so in my process of healing, I decided to change something besides my attitude. My girls had known me as Nova for years and called me that from time to time anyway. It was my pledge name back in college. It means "newness" and with all I'd been through, that was the best time to make it official.

"Girl, what the hell are you over there thinking about? You have been staring off in space for a good five minutes," Ziva said, rolling her eyes.

It was our monthly girl's time. We were at Jade's house this month. Jade decided that she wanted it to be a Mexican theme, so we had steak tacos, chicken enchiladas, tortillas and dip, yellow rice, mini chimichangas and of course, my favorite, Tequila margaritas. I was ready to fuck up some real food. I had been on a liquid diet for over two months during my ordeal. It took a couple more weeks for me to feel comfortable biting down on anything, but now I feel great and it's about to be on.

Ziva was sitting on the loveseat stuffing her face, Jade, like me was sitting indian style on the floor drinking a margarita, and Monica was scrolling through her phone laying on the couch. The four of us had been friends since college. Monica and Jade, who are known as Mo and Jae at times, were my roomates the entire four years. We did everything together, becoming like sisters.

That was good for me because I didn't' have any siblings. All I had was my parents at the time. Ziva has beeb around much longer, but I love them all the same. The three of them were my support when my parents died and it only brought us closer.

"Nothing really. I'm good." I tried to downplay my mood.

"We are not gonna have that moping shit going on today, hunni. We are here to have a good time. We haven't hung out and had fun in a long time. We were trying to keep you in a good place these last few months and we succeeded. Let's enjoy ourselves with some of this good food and some drinks. Then maybe we can hit the club being that it's Friday and still early as hell," Jade added her input.

"Y'all know Nova's ass ain't trying to go no damn where. She was over there thinking about that nigga, Kelvin. Tell me I'm wrong. I'll wait." Ziva said, popping a tortilla in her mouth and rolling her eyes.

"If I wanted you to know what I was thinking about, I would've told your ass. But it's just like you to assume some shit. Haven't you been taught that if you assume something you make an ass out of yourself? Stay out my business unless I invite you to it, Z," I stated, letting her know that I wasn't with her shit today.

"Excuse the fuck out of me! I was just trying to get you to talk the shit out since you are staying mute about it. I thought we were better than that and held no secrets, but I guess I thought wrong," she said with much attitude, getting up from the loveseat and walked to the kitchen.

See, Ziva has been throwing a lot of shade these last couple of months. She is so damn messy with it, too, so I had to put her in her place. She was pissed off because I hadn't given her the details of what happened to me. Our relationship had become distant at a very rapid pace, because of her slick ass mouth.

She lived her life through others because she refused to get her shit in order. She waited for a nigga to do something for her, instead of going out to get it on her own. You can lead a horse to water, but you can't make that muthafucka drink it. That's Ziva though. I kept my eyes open because I sensed the disloyalty within her. I just couldn't pinpoint it right now. But every donkey had its day and she better hope she wasn't on no ruthless shit.

Monica had been sitting back, soaking everything in. She didn't like when Ziva was in her moods. But she, too, suspected her of being foul as she opted to just watch her sneaky ass. She selected a station on Pandora and turned the volume up, drowning out the bullshit, it was time to party. Ciara's "Body Party" started playing and we all jumped up. Ziva hurried out the kitchen, and started dancing and acting silly. That was how I liked to have a good time. All that other mess was forgotten about for the time being.

***

We all decided that we would hit this club called The G Spot. It just opened about a month ago and I heard that was the place to be for a night of fun. Deciding to meet up at my house at eleven, everyone headed out to get dressed.

Pulling up to my house, I gathered my purse and opened the door. I hit the alarm on my car and walked up to the door. There was no need to park in the garage because I was heading back out. I unlocked the door and turned on the lights, making my way to my bedroom to find something to wear. Not in the mood to get all spiffy, I decided on an off the shoulder olive green blouse, a pair of tight skinny jeans with my olive green Dolce & Gabbana stilettos.

Once I got my outfit in order, I made my way into the bathroom to shower. As I was about to step in, I heard my phone ringing.

"Who the hell can this be?" I asked myself, irritated as hell.

Picking up the phone, I saw that it was Kelvin calling. Not even about to entertain the bullshit, I placed the phone back on the nightstand. *I know he didn't think he was gonna talk to me after what the fuck he did. Shit, I couldn't talk for a long ass time after that, so pretend my jaws are still wired shut muthafucka.*

My phone rang a couple more times, followed by banging on my door. I knew at that moment that Kelvin was at my door. I didn't have time for this tonight. I ignored all that noise and got in the shower. I washed my body and got out, wrapping myself in a plush bath towel. I entered my bedroom and low and behold, this nigga was sitting on my bed.

"Kelvin, how—how did you get in my house?" I stuttered.

"You didn't get the hint when I didn't respond to your calls, or the way you were banging on my door?"

I was scared as hell, and I tried not to show it. But I knew that I had to check myself because there was no way I'd be able to get to my gun.

"It doesn't matter how I got in this muthafucka, I'm in. I'm gonna let you know one more time when I call, you answer. I don't give a damn what you got going on. Is that understood?"

This nigga done lost his rabbit ass mind. How does he expect a muthafucka to talk with wires holding their jaws together? That's the stupidest shit I'd ever heard.

"You do know that I have been living my life as a mute the last few months, right? Thanks to you, putting your hands on me like I was a fuckin' man. I don't want to talk to you after that shit! You and I are not together. We will never be *together* ever again. You showed me that night what you thought of me. You told me out your own mouth how you felt about me. So, my question to you is, why are you even here? I mean you just broke in my damn house like that was cool. This is not gonna be like it was in the past. You do what the hell you want to do, get caught, then everything is good. It's a new day, baby boy. Ain't none of that. I would appreciate if you would leave before I call the po—"

Before I could get the word "police" out, he had both of his hands around my neck, squeezing with all his might with a raging expression on his face.

"Bitch, you must've forgot who the fuck I am! Yeah, I beat yo' ass and left you there, but you were coming at me the same way you're doing now. I can come back whenever the fuck I choose to. Now again, when I call yo' ass you better answer. You still belong to me and the minute you realize that shit, life will be much easier for you."

He pushed me back with so much force that I hit the corner of the dresser. I yelped out and held my right side. It had to be bruised badly because I was in excruciating pain. This was the second time this muthafucka had put his hands on me. I guess because I didn't press charges on his ass, he felt like I would continue to take this shit. But that's not the case. He didn't know that he was about to unleash a side of me that he didn't want to see.

I'm not gonna lie, the nigga still scared the hell out me and that was the reason I didn't try to jump bad. I didn't want to say anything to make him kick my ass, so I just kept my mouth closed. Not knowing what he would do next was frightening.

He got up off my bed and walked towards me. I flinched when he pulled me in, hugged me and kissed my forehead. My skin crawled from his touch.

"I'll see you around, remember what I said. You are mine. Don't get no ideas about going out shakin' yo ass, meeting the next nigga. I'll kill that muthafucka," he said with a sinister grin on his face. This man was crazy as fuck and he had me shook.

Kelvin left out of the front door and had the nerve to lock it behind himself. He had a duplicate key to my shit! It was now ten-thirty and I still needed to get dressed. I'm not gonna let him ruin my night, but I will be getting those locks changed first thing in the morning.

Chapter 3
Ziva

This hit, that ice cold
Michelle Pfeiffer, that white gold.
This one for them hood girls
Them good girls' straight masterpieces
Stylin', whilen, livin' it up in the city
Got Chucks on with Saint Laurent
Gotta kiss myself, I'm so pretty.

I was jammin' to Bruno Mars's, "Uptown Funk", while getting ready to hit the streets with my girls. I looked at myself in the mirror, and couldn't do nothing but smile at my reflection. I ran my fingers through my twist while applying oil to them.

"Yep, I know I'm a pretty bitch," I said, blowing a kiss to myself. My outfit for tonight was a red bodycon dress that was hugging all my curves just right, gold accessories with my gold Jimmy Choo heels. I had a fresh manicure and my hair was laid. I supply the hook to reel these niggas in every time.

I couldn't help myself, thinking about the slick shit Nova said earlier, but I let her have it. That's my girl, but she better pipe down. It's not my fault that Kelvin beat the fuck out her. Yeah, I knew what happened even though she didn't tell me. She need to learn how to talk to a nigga and shut the fuck up on cue.

I guess she found her inner bad ass at the wrong time and he put them paws on her ass. But when a bitch deal with a nigga that's dragging them through the mud and keeps forgiving him, he's gonna run with that shit. Ain't no leaving, dummy. He feels he owns your ass after that, but a bitch like me would've had his ass locked up, no hesitations.

I was her cheerleader, letting her cry on my shoulder, but I don't have any sympathy for her. She should have been kicked him to the curb. He came through when he wanted to, had clothes at her crib like he lived there but got a whole crib of his own that she didn't know anything about. But they were engaged. Yeah okay.

I'd told her many times that she needed to love herself, but she wasn't trying to hear me. I refused to come straight out to let her know that he wasn't shit, he showed her on his own daily. It was up to her to make a choice and her choice was to stay with him. So, I did what I was supposed to do, I held out some tissue when she needed it.

I threw a lot in her face just to piss her off. I did it because even though she had her jaws clamped together for months, the bitch didn't have any blemishes and was still cute. I know I sound like a hater, but I wanted to see some type of deformities.

I knew many people questioned our friendship back in the day, but if Nova wasn't saying nothing I was cool. What other's thought didn't bother me at all. We'd been rockin' together too long to let that come in between us. Nova and I graduated high school together and even went to the same college, but my hot ass let the streets and the dope boys cloud my judgement and dropped out.

Dealing with one mediocre job after another, I couldn't compete with her if I tried. She did everything she was supposed to do, and that's why she is still in the same career field she went to school for. It's not her fault that I fucked up, but I feel like she didn't even try to encourage me to do better. All she knew how to do was throw her money around like she was mega rich or something.

Nova helped me on many occasions, but I never asked her for nothing, she owed me every dime. Whenever anything went down with her, I was there. When Kelvin was doing her dirty, cheating and fucking anything that would spread their legs, I was there. She was weak for his ass, but I guess it got old because she ain't studying him.

But if she new half of what was going down the four years they were together, she would fall dead on the spot. I tolerated that bitch, but her life is not gonna be golden if I have anything to do with it.

I collected everything that I was gonna need for the night, disconnected my phone from the charger and left out the door. I jumped in my ride, connected my phone to the Bluetooth. With the music blasting, I pulled off in route to Nova's crib.

When I pulled up, I noticed that everyone was already there. The four of us had been rocking for years, but I knew they low key talked about my ass at times. I didn't have a good job or a career. Shit, I didn't even have a college education, but so what. I lived my life the way I saw fit. It didn't matter if I used niggas to get what I needed. It worked for me, but they knew better than to throw anything up in my face.

I got out the car looking like the diva I set out to be and rung the bell. Jade opened the door with a fake ass smile on her face. This one here I knew was low key jealous of me.

"It's about time you made it. We was waiting for you." She gave me a fake ass hug and pulled back.

"You're lookin' good, boo! That dress is hot!" she said, stepping back checking me out.

"You ain't gotta tell me what I already know, hunni, but thanks." I said and rolled my eyes. I know I was being very extra, but so the fuck what. I don't like phony, so I don't sugarcoat at all. I spoke my mind.

Monica and Nova walked out the back room laughing and shit.

"What's so funny? I wanna laugh, too," I said with my hand on my hip.

"Girl, it was nothing, Mo was talking about how my ass is suffocating in these jeans," she laughed.

"I don't know why you are wearing jeans to the club anyway. You're trying to find a man, right? I would say show a little bit more and make them niggas flock to you." I was serious as hell about that shit.

"You're showing a lot more for all of us put together. I'm good with what I have on, thank you." Nova rolled her eyes and walked to the mini bar in her dining room.

"I'm just trying to let you know you are not gonna find a man dressed like you are. I'm trying to help you." I followed her into the room and took a seat on one of the barstools.

Monica looked at both of us but focused mainly on me. "I don't know what's been going on with you as of late, but you have this bitterness about you. Think about what you say before you say it," Monica said, walking away.

"I don't know what the problem is shit, I pointed out the obvious. She ain't getting no man dressed like that period. I'm gonna sit back and mind my business though. Is that better, *Monica?*" I asked, stretching her name with every syllable.

She only looked at me, rolling her eyes. This friendship with these three is just about over. There wasn't any getting around it. They dictated too much about what I did in my life. I'm grown, but I guess they forgot that part.

"Let's take a shot before we go. We need to ease the tension that's in the room," said Monica who always tried to be the peacemaker.

"There isn't any tension. Ya'll just making shit out to be more than it was. But it's all good, muthafuckas need to just get out of their feelings," I said, walking to the mini bar.

No one said anything in response to what I said and that was the best thing to do. Monica poured the shots and each of us grabbed one. We held up the glasses and in unison said, "Bad Bitches!" before throwing the shots back.

"I think that we all should ride in my truck. What do y'all think?" Jade asked, looking around after drinking some water.

I didn't want to ride with them, so I opted to drive my own car. Good thing there wasn't any rebuttal from any of them.

"If that's what you wanna do, so be it. Let's go," Nova said, walking out the door.

***

Club GSpot was very elegant, but hood at the same time. When we walked in, there was a long bar straight ahead stocked with every type of alcoholic beverage that's on the market. Then there was a huge dance floor in the center of the room surrounded by plush seats. Some of the seats were arranged in semicircles throughout the place. There was also a small bar in the back and VIP was upstairs.

I was looking around, scoping out the place. There were many men that were fine different varieties of men and women in this spot. I just had to figure out who had what I wanted: money. That's all I cared about.

We made our way to the main bar to order drinks and my jam blasted throughout the club. Yo Gotti's "Rake It Up" had me twerkin' my ass to every beat that dropped. I saw the whole club stop what they were doing to watch.

I tell all my hoes; rake it up
Break it down, back it up
Fuck it up, fuck it up
Back it up, back it up
Rake it up, rake it up
Back it up, back it up

And backed that ass up I did. I could dance my ass off, especially if it was to get a nigga's attention. There were plenty of them watching all this ass, too. It's true what they say. You dance how you fuck. At least it's true for me. I don't know about the other bitches.

I felt somebody behind me, all on my ass. I looked over my shoulder and there stood a nigga that was fine as hell. The only problem was, this dude looked like three years ago. His clothes were outdated, shoes were scuffed the fuck up and his pockets didn't have a bulge at all. But shid, he had a bulge in the front of his pants though. That wasn't the point. He wasn't paid, so that would be a no for me.

The song ended and I made my way to the bar with my girls. Ole boy was right behind me. I sat down and waited to order my drink. The waitress came over and I asked, "Can I get a double shot of Patron, please?"

"Sure, I'll be right back," she said with a smile. She was cheesing hard for a tip she wasn't gonna get.

She came back with my drink and dude was like "I got it, ma", peeling a twenty from his small stash.

"Nah, you don't have to do that. I can pay for my own drink," I stated without turning around, after I saw how much money was in his hand.

"It's only right to take care of a beautiful woman," he pressed.

"You can't afford me, hun. Put ya money back in your pocket and leave me alone. There's nothing you can do for me," I said, turning to look him in his face as I spoke.

The look on his face said it all. He was madder than that thang, but I didn't care. He had to come with more than a big dick. I'm glad he just turned and walked away because I didn't feel like acting a fool at that point. Shit, I just got here.

Chapter 4
Monica

This club was jumpin'! There were so many fine brothers in the building. If it was meant for me to find a man tonight, so be it, but I wasn't looking. His ass would have to find me. I'd been single for three years and I'm happy. I can't open my heart up to just anyone. These men out here today would play with your heart like it's a spades hand and I don't have time for the bull.

I'm twenty-six, 5'7", one hundred and seventy pounds, dark skinned and beautiful. I recently lost thirty-five pounds and I'm loving myself more everyday.

I was in a relationship with a man that put me down every chance he got, which was everyday I was in his presence. He beat my self esteem into the ground. But when I caught him in my bed with the next hoe, I tried to kill both of their asses. I bet he will think twice about fucking a bitch in the next woman's house. Let's just say he knows how Al Green felt when them hot ass grits stuck to his skin. I play with a lot of things, but disrespect is not one of them.

That's why I was looking at Ziva crazy. She just dissed that dude and made him look like shit on the bottom of her shoe. Sometimes I can't stand her. She is so evil at times. All she had to do was say "no thanks" and leave it at that, but *noooo* she had to do the most like she is living the luxury life. If I had anything to say about it, she should have let him pay for that damn drink. Besides, before the night is out, she will be mooching off Nova with her broke ass.

I don't understand how a woman can be content with waiting for a man to do everything for her. But if she like it, I loved it. I couldn't stand the way she basically used Nova, but she saw it as helping a friend. No, dammit. She needed to file her on her taxes as a dependent.

"Did y'all see that broke muthafucka trying to get close to me? His ass had forty-three dollars in his pocket, trying to buy a bitch a drink." Ziva laughed hard as hell because of the way that she played that man.

"Z, why did you have to say all of that to him? All you had to do was say 'no thanks' and leave it alone. That was foul as hell," I said to her.

"If you feel I was wrong, you go pacify that nigga. *I don't do broke nothing!* And all y'all know this," she replied, irritably. She took a sip from her glass and got up to go to the dance floor.

I looked at her until she disappeared into the crowd. That's what she does, runs away when no one agrees with the way she acts or the things she says.

"She's gonna meet her match one of these days," I said to no one in particular.

What she didn't understand was we knew the real her, she didn't have to front for us. *We* knew that she was the "broke" that she didn't do.

"Mo, you already know that Z hasn't changed in all this time she won't. She has her preference and you can't make her do right." There Jade ass goes trying to play the reasoner.

"Yes, you're correct right there. She hasn't changed and that's her problem. She's not in college anymore, so it's about time for her to grow up. She is so damn irresponsible and thinks everyone is supposed to clean up her fuck ups. That's not how life works, but she will learn the hard way for sure."

We sat watching how everyone was enjoying themselves on the dance floor until the converstion about Ziva came to a halt. If we continued to talk about her and her ways, it would"ve spoiled the night. The mood changed when the DJ started playing a juke mix and the crowd went wild. We jumped up and started dancing where we stood.

During our juke session, a group of niggas entered the club. I was lowkey watching them from the time they entered, and they were all fine. They were dressed well and carried themselves like bosses. Every one of them had on tailored suits and expensive ass shoes. I loved a man that looked good in a suit, these men were distinguished gentlemen.

This made me pop my ass even harder while dancing. Yes, lawd, I was trying to get lucky that tonight. I looked out the side of my eye and saw the group coming our way. I didn't know if the others saw what I was seeing, but I refused to make it obvious that I was checking for them. They all got comfortable at the bar not too far from where we were and they were enjoying the show.

Nova was getting freaky to the song "Freaky Muthafuckas" all by herself. She was gyrating her hips like she was riding a dick, hittin' it, too. She danced her ass off without trying.

We all went crazy when "I Wanna Fuck You in the Azz" by the Outhere Brothers, another old school Chitown favorite, came on. Every woman in the building had her ass in the air when that beat dropped. Niggas knew what time it was. They stood back with drinks in hand, watching the room full of booty of all sizes bounce around.

When the song ended, we returned to our seats laughing and giving each other high-fives on how we had just showed out. We were having a good time and we all needed it.

"Girl, I haven't danced like that in a long time! That brought back so many memories. My knees are gonna be hurting like a muthafucka tomorrow," Jade laughed, wiping the sweat from her face.

We used to dance like that every weekend at the clubs when we were in college, so it was good to let our hair down but it wasn't over. "Back to Sleep" came on as the DJ slowed it down a bit. This was Nova's song and she didn't need a soul on the dance floor with her to do what she did best. She made her way to the the floor and fucked it up alone.

She was out there with all eyes on her. The way her body moved seemed like she was one of those video vixens that was chosen to dance. One of the guys from the group that came in earlier stood up, and admired her from afar. He started walking towards her with so much swag and confidence, licking his lips with every step. This man positioned himself behind her, picking up the beat with no problem.

Nova didn't look back to see who it was, she just kept dancing. They were moving their bodies in unison like they had been dancing together forever. She finally turned around to see who was dancing with her. The way he looked at her, made me think they were about to get their freak on right there on the dance floor. Their moves were synced and on point.

When Nova turned, and started gyrating on his dick, I thought he was gonna cum on the spot. He grabbed her hand and she spinned out on cue. Then they walked it out together without thinking about it. Meeting back up in the middle, her legs spreaded slightly while he ran his hands up her thighs. That shit looked very sensual.

I cheered my bitch on with that shit. The song ended and they left the dance floor hand in hand. They walked back to the bar where me and Jade was sitting, smiling at one another. He pulled out her seat and sat next to her. I hadn't seen her smile like that in a very long time.

Chapter 5
Nova

I was on the floor getting my dance on. I loved this song so much, it's like I turn into an entirely different person whenever I'm dancing. I feel so free when my body is doing what it wants. Zoned out, I felt a pair of strong hands on the small of my back. When I turned smoothly to the beat, I saw the most beautiful sight moving to my beat with me. It's been awhile since any man could keep up with me on the dance floor. I was excited on the inside because I needed to see if he could keep up.

I moved my body very sensually on purpose and that nigga was right there with me. My heart was pounding with pride. We danced the entire song like we practiced that number before hitting the club. I didn't know this man from a can of paint, but I'm not disappointed. No, not at all and he wasn't hard one my eyes either. His lips alone were saying kiss me and I almost did it, too.

I had to turn my back to him because my love box was about to erupt. I started grinding on his stick and Lord knows I leaked all in my thong. I was relieved when he spun me out. If I stayed on his python, we would've tried to find a dark corner to put out this fire.

When the song ended, no words were spoken. He just led me to my seat by my hand as we smiled at each other the entire way. He was such a gentleman, proving there were still some out there that knew how to court a woman. He then pulled out my barstool and made sure I was comfortable.

Waving down the bartender, I asked, "Would you get me a double shot of 1800 and a half glass of pineapple juice, please?"

"Sure thing, hun," she said.

"Excuse me, ma. Put their drinks on my tab for the night," he said to the bartender before she left to make my drink.

"No problem, boss."

This mystery man stood by my side, staring a hole through the side of my face. I looked over and all he did was smile. He had the prettiest teeth, his eyes were green and lips were pink as ever. I looked away just to get my focus back.

"Is there anything you want to say to me? I mean you do know that it's not polite to stare, right?" I said flirtatiously.

Hell yeah, I was flirting! This man was fine! And he matched my moves, so I knew that he was great in bed. That thought alone made me blush.

"I just wanted to tell you how beautiful I think you are. I know you hear it all the time, but you haven't heard it from me, so there's a difference," he said, licking his lips.

"Thank you." That's all my mind would allow me to say. I had never beeen tongue-tied until that moment.

"So, what's your name, Miss Lady? I mean, if you don't mind me asking." There he goes, licking them lips just like LL Cool J. My eyes couldn't do anything but follow the trail that his tongue made along his lips.

"Ummm, ummm. I'm sorry. What did you say? My mind kind of took me someplace else," I said, shaking my head chuckling.

"It's cool," he said with a smirk on his face. "I asked what's your name, sweetie."

"I'm Nova. Nice to meet you and you are?" I asked, looking him dead in his gorgeous eyes. It's like I was being hypnotized by them because I couldn't break away even though I tried.

"Nova, that's unique. Your parents didn't want you to have a name that someone else was rockin', huh? But I like it." He grabbed my hand and brought it to his lips.

"My name is Grant, but everyone calls me G. Nice to meet you. Is there a meaning to your name?"

He was rubbing his thumb along my knuckles. That small gesture had me ready to lay him down and give him every inch of my body. I hadn"t been touched by a man in months and my inner self was screaming at me to make it happen.

"My parents actually named me Sabrina. I changed my name to Nova a couple of months ago when I changed other things in my life. But that's a story for another day."

At that moment, the bartender came back with my drink. I took some money out of my clutch to tip her. But he shut that down quickly.

"You're good, baby girl. Everything is on me."

He took the money from my hand and placed it back in my clutch. I wasn't going to argue with this man. I like a man that still knows how to treat a lady as such.

"Thanks, again. I appreciate that. I'll have to take you out and return the favor." I took a sip from my glass and started playing with the straw.

"That's the second time you hinted at being in my presence sometime in the future. Are you trying to ask me out or something, Miss Nova?"

This man had the sexiest smile and he had deep dimples. I love a man with dimples. *I could just—* I thought before I stopped myself. *Slow down now, Nova. Get yourself together, girl!*

Taking a deep breath, I said, "It won't be a date or anything like that. Just going out and having some fun. You know, get to know each other a little."

My face was hot and I knew I was blushing like a little school girl. My throat was instantly dry at that point, so I picked up the glass of pineapple juice, taking a long sip.

"Where's your phone? Let me see it?"

I already knew what he was about to do, I reached in my clutch and handed him my iPhone 7. He pushed the home button, entered his number and pressed the telephone icon. His phone rang and he pulled it from his hip and silenced it.

"Now you can reach me at any time, beautiful. When you're ready, just hit me up," he said, handing me back my phone.

He looked down at his phone and punched a series of buttons and put it away. "Now you're locked in with me, as well, but we have plenty of time to talk later. For now, let's show these folks how to dance."

He stood and held out his hand. "May I have this dance, Miss Nova?"

Taking his hand, we made our way to the dance floor.

Chapter 6
G

When I saw shawty on the dance floor with her girls, I couldn't take my eyes off her. She was having so much fun and didn't seem to have a care in the world. She was about 5'5", a hundred fifty, maybe sixty pounds, caramel complexion, bouncy curly hair and enough ass and hips for me to get a firm grip. I loved the way she moved. She had me stuck.

"Damn, G, lil' mama got ya ass over here damn near needing a bib for that dribble that's about to fall from ya lip," my nigga, Scony, said cracking the fuck up.

"Shid, she is bad, nigga. I ain't gon' lie, I was watching her ass, too," Scony added.

"But did you check out her girl though, with her chocolate ass? That's the one I'm going after." My cousin Antonio loved him some dark-skinned women, when he set out to get one, oh he's gonna get her.

"I got that one, brah. You can look but you won't get the opportunity to touch. That's all me right there, playa," I said, continuing to watch her body movements.

We sat there choppin' it up, getting our drink on watchin these ladies enjoy themselves.

I couldn't take my eyes off baby girl at all. The way her bod moved had a nigga zoned out.

"G, you good, bro? Yo' ass haven't stopped eying shorty since she hit the floor. Don't let me find out she got ya ass and you haven't even introduced yo'self yet. Over there lookin' a lil' thirsty my nigga. That shit right there is making you look soft as fuck." Scony cracked up.

"Nigga, yo' ass out of all people know aint't shit soft about me! Don't get jaw jacked muthafucka," I laughed and swung on him in a playful manner.

See, I use to be a street nigga, but the streets ain't for me. Don't get it twisted, a nigga still gets down with the best of them. I just put my best man in the front and I ride the back. We still get this money, legally and illegally. When I eat, everybody eats. My team is strong and we are maintaining this shit. I needed to shut this nigga Scony up by giving a lesson on how to approach a woman and I wasn't leaving without making my presence known.

The DJ changed the mood and "Back To Sleep" came on. Baby girl glided to the dance floor, that must be her shit. Her body was moving like she was a slithering snake and I was the man blowing the pungi to get her out of the woven basket. I topped off my drink and made my way over to her.

"This nigga on his mack shit," I heard Antonio say as I walked to the dance floor.

There weren't any words needed, our bodies spoke for us. We took over the floor as all eyes were on us. I was surprised she kept up with me. That was very rare in today's dance styles. These women only knew how to make that ass pop. This is the moment to take notes.

Classy dancing still gets noticed out here and this woman was in a class of her own. When we finished, we headed back to the bar. She ordered a drink and we talked. It dawned on me at that moment that she and her friends didn't get giddy over me and my guys. There are bitches standing around gawking and shit as I speak.

I introduced myself to her, but she didn't flinch or get excited hearing my name. That tells me she didn't know who I was. Hell, she didn't know my name until I told her. Yeah, that's the type of woman I need on my arm, someone that don't look at my status. One that's gonna learn who I am and not how much money I have. I like her style, but she is always holding her head down. She has a story to tell, but I won't pry until she mentions it. After awhile, I wanted to be close to her again, so I asked her to dance with me.

The dance floor was packed. I already knew that me and baby girl was about to open that bitch up a little bit. When the boss comes on the floor, they already knew. We were having a good time dancing and acting silly. I loved a woman that could let loose and enjoy herself.

"Wild Thoughts" came on and I saw this woman morph right before my eyes. She was so serious when she danced to songs that she obviously loved. We were stepping and spinning all around that floor. We complimented each other very well. I was trying to keep my mind off how she may perform in bed. I wasn't trying to jump her bones just yet, but I had plans of her ass moaning in my ear in the future.

My club was packed that night. Yes, Gspot is my baby. A lot of people showed up to have a good time and that's exactly what was going on at that very moment. The lights were dimmed low and the music was bangin'. You could see people mouths moving, singing the lyrics to the song, but the music was blasted high and that's all that was heard. The DJ was hyping us up with every track he played. I closed my eyes briefly, I was taking in all my success when all hell broke loose.

A series of gunshots rang out and the sound of people screaming and scrambling could be heard. Nova's body fell into me like she was trying to duck. I was trying to see where the shots were coming from, but there were so many. After saying a quick prayer, the shots stopped suddenly. People were trying to get out of the club, which wasn't a problem because there were at least five ways to get out. Especially since there was only one way to get into the club for security reasons.

"Ok, baby girl, I think it's cool. Let me take you back to your girls so I can see what's going on."

I tried to lift her up, but she cried out. "I got hit., My head hurts, G," she said through her sobs. I bent down the moment the lights came on. She had tears running down her face along with a flow of blood, that was coming from the left side of her head. At that moment, Scony came running towards me.

"The police and ambulance is on the way, my nigga. There's about thirteen people that got shot, but nothing serious," he said calmly, but stern.

"Fourteen. Lil' mama got hit on the left side of her head. Don't try to move, sweetie. Stay still."

I started searching through her hair on the side that I saw the blood coming from. I couldn't find a wound, but there was lots of blood. Then I saw some of her hair was missing, so. I parted her hair and there was a gash on the side of her head. She was a very lucky woman. She was only grazed by that non-shooting muthafucka', but she was bleeding a lot. I grabbed the handkerchief from my breast pocket and applied pressure, trying to stop the bleeding.

"I just met you, but I'm not trying to let you go just yet. So be still for me, baby."

"Damn, man, let me go see if the ambulance is outside. Tonio and the rest of the crew along with security is manning the crowd. Quan is pulling the tapes," he said, filling me in on what was going down, then left to get help.

I saw her girls talking to Scony, I guess telling them what was going on. Then he pointed in our direction. I looked down and baby girl opened her eyes and said, "Why me, G?" Then she lost consciousness.

Chapter7
Ziva

I had to get away from my so-called friends before I slapped one of them. They always have something to say about what I did. I had been the same from day one, nothing had changed about me. Now suddenly, it's a problem with everything I did or said. The distance between us was out there for all to see, but I don't give a fuck though! I wasn't about to act as if I was having a good time when I knew that wasn't the case.

I left them sitting at the bar and I went to find someone that could add to my bank account. I didn't come to the club to sit around and watch people. I liked to be seen. I ran into this guy that I knew from around the way named Conte. We were talking and catching up when I looked up and peeped Nova dancing with this fine ass dude. I stared a little harder. My face scowled from recognition alone as I got mad instantly.

See, I knew all about that nigga, G. He is paid but he wants to be all in her Simple Simon ass face. But that shit will be short lived since I'm about to throw a monkey wrench in her night. I know what I'm about to do is wrong, but oh well, she can't win them all.

I grabbed my phone out of my purse and unlocked it. "Damn, ma, you just gonna text a muthafucka' while I'm talking to you?" Conte said with much attitude.

I forgot his ass was standing there to be honest. Once I saw that Nova was wheeling in a big fish, nothing else mattered.

"My bad. I felt my phone vibrate. It could be important, give me a minute." I looked up at him briefly and continued what I started. An idea popped in my head and I ran with it. I figured showing was better than telling, so I had to send a visual. I took a quick picture of Nova and G dancing. This is the picture I needed, a perfect shot. Now it was time for me to shoot this text to the one person that wouldn't think it was so cute.

 Me: *Aye, you should come on down to GSpot on Rush Street. Ya girl in rare form.*

I attached the photo and pressed send. The photo didn't have G's face in it, but it showed that they were very close to one another. But it was enough to make this nigga, Kelvin, go crazy.

 Kelvin: *I'm not far from there. Good lookin' out, shorty.*

This fool was head over heels for her ass, but she wanted nothing to do with him. Still, he would drop shit on a dime to be around her. I didn't understand what it was about her. Everybody treated her like she was royalty or some shit.

"So, what have you been up to, Z? I haven't seen you in a minute. I just got back home a few weeks ago."

Conte started talking to me again as he took my mind off what I had done. I used to fuck Conte back in the day, but his money wasn't long enough for me.

"I've been just chilling, trying to get me together, you know. What are you doing with yourself these days?"

"I'm running a lil' cleaning business back in Indiana. It's doing pretty well, too, but I had to come back home to see what was going on."

I tuned Conte out once I saw Kelvin step in the club with a mug on his face. It took him about fifteen minutes to get to the club. He was looking around, trying to spot Nova. I knew the exact moment when he did. It was crowded as hell in GSpot that night, but my eyes were only on him.

He pulled the gun from his waistband and put it close to his leg. I quickly shot a look at Nova to see what she was doing. She was dancing and smiling, not paying attention to anyone but G. She turned her back towards the direction where Kelvin was. At that moment, G wrapped her in his arms and ran his hand across her face. He whispered something in her ear that made her throw her head back and laughed. She then wrapped her arms around his neck and continued to dance.

"What's the matter with you, Z? You look like you saw a ghost?" Conte was trying to figure out what was up with me.

I looked at him briefly and my eyes darted back to Kelvin. Then I took off in the direction of Nova with Conte right behind me. I was praying to myself that he wouldn't do what I already thought when I saw the gun. There were so many people, I was having a hard time maneuvering my way through the crowd.

My heart was pounding because I didn't want him to shoot anyone. I just wanted him to show up and make a scene and embarrass her, nothing more. Tears blurred my vision as I pushed harder to get through, but I was too late. He started shooting before he even made it to her.

People started ducking, screaming, and running, trying to get out of the way and out of the club. I froze in the spot where I stood, frantically looking around, but I didn't see Nova anywhere. Now I did see Kelvin run out the closest exit door. Things were so chaotic that I kept getting pushed further and further back. Finally finding a path that opened, I headed in the direction my girls were earlier.

I finally made it to the spot where I saw Nova, Mo and Jade was already there. They were kneeling and that's when I knew Nova was hit.

"Oh my God! Is she ok? What the hell happened?" I screamed. "Nova, you're gonna be ok! Hang in there, sis!" I genuinely didn't want her to get hurt.

I looked up and the EMTs were being escorted our way to check out Nova and the people that had got hurt.

"Step the fuck back y'all so they can work on her!" G's voice boomed out and everyone parted like the Red Sea.

"Where was she shot?" the EMT asked.

"She was hit on the left side of her head. I didn't move her or allow her to move. I just put pressure on the wound. She lost consciousness about three minutes ago. It appears to be only a graze, but she has a deep gash." G said that shit like he was a fucking doctor or something.

"Please make sure she is ok, man," G begged.

This nigga didn't even know her and there he was ready to shed tears behind her. I know that wasn't the time to be jealous, but I couldn't help it. The EMTs put her on oxygen and started an IV line. Then they bandaged her head and put a brace on her neck to prevent her head from moving.

"It doesn't appear to be serious, but with a head injury you can't be too sure," the EMT stated.

Nova was rushed out of the building as they hurried to put her into the ambulance. Once we got outside, I saw there were about a dozen ambulance vehicles and just as many police cars outside the club.

"What hospital are you taking her to?" I asked.

"We will be taking her to Northwestern Memorial. Anyone riding with her? If so, let's go!" he yelled.

Mo's big ass jumped in the back with Nova while Jade ran to her car to follow behind the ambulance. While they took off, I had a call to make. This shit was all my fault.

Chapter 8
Monica

I was sitting in the ambulance while the EMT was working on one of best friends. I had to be there because we were the only family she had. Nova lost both of her parents two years ago after they were hit head on by a drunk driver. Her mom died on the scene and her dad died at the hospital. It took her a very long time to accept the fact that her parents were no longer here on earth.

Now here it was two years later and she was shot in the damn head. The EMT said it's not serious, but why hadn't she woken up yet? My nerves are all over the place right now.

"Ma'am, ma'am!" The EMT was screaming at me, bringing my thoughts to a halt.

"Yes, I'm sorry. What did you say?"

"Does she have any known allergies that we should know about? Any known health problems?" he asked in a much calmer voice.

"No, she's not allergic to anything at all. But a couple of months ago, she had surgery on her jaws and had them wired. Other than that, she's always been healthy," I said, answering his questions the best I could.

"Ok, thank you, ma'am," he said as he checked her vitals.

We finally made it to the hospital about five minutes later. They rushed her straight to the back without stopping. Jade came through the hospital doors walking full speed. She was throwing question after question at me, but I didn't have the answers to any of them.

"Calm down, Jade. They just took her to the back. It's too soon to report anything. That's all I know right now," I said with tears in my eyes.

"We were having such a good time, then everything went into another direction. I was scared as hell from the gunshots alone, Mo. Then to find out one of my best friends was shot..." Jade stopped talking and started crying so hard that her body shook uncontrollably.

"Calm down, Jade. She's gonna be alright. I promise, she will be okay. Nova is strong, she has so much more life to live. We have to get ourselves together because when we go back there to see her, we have to be strong for her." I spoke out loud to comfort Jade, but I had to coach myself to believe what I had said as well.

The automatic doors to the hospital opened again, and in walked the guy from the club and his friends. He had a look on his face like he was ready to kill someone. I didn't understand why because he didn't even know us like that.

"Hey, y'all. How is she doing?" he asked, walking to where we were seated.

"They rushed her to the back, but they haven't given us an update yet," I replied.

He sat down in an empty chair and started staring off into space. It seemed like something was weighing heavily on his mind. When he looked up at me, his eyes had gone from green to a dark hazel color. I heard that people with those pretty ass eyes can show what mood they were in by the change in color. It was a beautiful sight though.

"Miss Lady—" he started speaking, but I cut him off.

"Sorry for interrupting you, but I'm Monica and this is Jade. We don't have to be formal around here," I said, trying to make light of the situation.

"Okay, nice to meet y'all. I'm Grant, but ya'll can call me G. That's Scony and Antonio."

We all said our hellos and G started talking again.

"I don't want to get all in baby girl's business, but is there someone that's out to hurt her?" G asked that question as if he knew something that we didn't.

"She was in a relationship with this guy, but she hasn't been dealing with him for months. I don't know if I should be telling you this because it's not my business to tell."

"Look, Monica, I need to know, shorty. See, I own GSpot and I looked at the footage with my own eyes. The nigga that shot that gun, pointed that muthafucka straight at her head. I couldn't see his face because it was dark, but I would bet my life that he was trying to kill her. Now I'm gonna ask you again, is there anyone that would want to hurt her?"

I looked over at Jade and she nodded her head for me to tell him what I knew.

"She was dating this guy named Kelvin Banks for about four years. She finally got tired of his bullshit and told him to leave. He beat her up a couple months ago and broke her jaw. They had to wire her jaws together, but she recently had the wires removed." G had fire in his eyes after he heard what happened to Nova.

"You mean to tell me that this nigga was beating on her?" he asked, staring me in my face waiting on my reply.

"From my understanding, that was the first time he had ever put his hands on her, but he's been disrespecting the relationship from the start. She had never said anything about him hitting her until that night."

"I can't stand a nigga that uses a female as a damn punching bag! Where do this nigga live or work at?" This man was mad as hell.

"Once he moved out of Nova's house, we don't know where he's been. But he has been poppin' up at her house, threatening her and calling her constantly. She told us about a month ago she's scared of him. She went to the Illinois Concealed Carry Firearm Training classes, so she's licensed to carry and owns a 9mm handgun. She goes to the range three to four times a week, so she's not afraid to use it."

"At least she is preparing to shoot that nigga if it comes down to it. She said something to me before she lost consciousness. She said, 'why me, G'. Now I know why she said it." G paused and shook his head repeatedly.

"He's gonna kill that nigga, Mo. Look how mad he is," Jade said, she tried to whisper in my ear, but it was an epic fail.

"I'm not gonna kill his ass just yet baby girl, but I'm gonna whoop his ass and show him what it feels like to beat a muthafucka like a man." G had ears like a damn lion because Jae wasn't even that loud.

"Somebody needs to whoop his ass. This is ridiculous. He needs to just leave her alone. It's obvious she don't want to have any dealings with him."

I couldn't stand his ass, so I didn't care what happened to him. I looked up and met the eyes of Antonio looking at me.

"Are you ok, Monica?" he asked, walking over to me and held out his hand. "Let's take a walk. I wanna make sure you're ok and get to know you while we wait."

I placed my hand in his and looked at Jade. She nodded her head yes for me to go.

"You don't have to worry about her. Scony will make sure she's alright," Antonio said, nodding at his boy.

"She will be alright here with us. I will make sure nothing happens to her," Scony said, as he got up and sat in a chair next to Jade. "I will also make sure you get a call if we hear anything while ya'll is gone."

We walked out of the hospital and Antonio hit the the alarm on his 2017 charcoal grey BMW. When we made it to the car, he opened my door and made sure I was in and shut the door. I reached over and opened his door for him. He paused and I heard him let out a low chuckle. He got in the car and started up and pulled off.

We decided to go to this all night breakfast spot on Roosevelt called White Palace. They had the best breakfast food in my opinion. It was now almost four in the morning and I didn't realize how hungry I was. Antonio ordered food for us as well as everyone back at the hospital. We had a little minute to wait before the order would be ready, so we sat and got to know each other a bit.

"What's your story, Monica? I know that you love your girls, now tell me about you."

This man was staring at me so hard, I felt like he was trying to see my inner soul.

"I'm single, if that's what you are wondering. I've been by myself for the past three years and it's been working for me so far. Yes, Nova and Jade are like my sisters and I love them. We are all we got."

"Well, how can I get to know you? I really like the way that you carry yourself. What do you do as far as your career?"

"It's not hard to get know me, just be you. If you are serious about getting to know me, everything will fall in place as the time goes by. That type of thing can't be rushed and I'm all for a new friendship."

"Okay, I feel you on that. We can take things slow and see where it goes," he said, never taking his eyes off me. "Now what do you do for work?"

"I'm a senior computer analyst. I'm doing very well for myself. I love my job. I've worked for the same company for the last five years. I started as an intern while still in college. When I graduated, I was offered a permanent position. I worked my ass off to get where I am today. What is it that you do?"

I looked into his eyes, which were different shades of brown. They weren't as mesmerizing as G's, but they were close.

"I own my own locksmith company in Atlanta called Davenport Locks. I'm considering opening another one here. I came to Chicago to help my cuzzo with his businesses. These niggas up here are grimey and there's nothing like family to have ya back. I've been here for six months, but the way it's looking I'll be here a little longer." He paused for a minute, shaking his head.

"I've never seen my cuz care about a female so quick like he does with ya girl. I'm gonna let you know now, dude fucked up doing baby girl like that. G don't like that shit at all. Shit I don't either. We had a situation where one of our female cousins was in this exact predictament. She didn't tell any of us about it. The muthafucka ended up killing her. Let's just say, the nigga didn't make it to trial. That messed all of us up, so that's the reason G is going so hard for her."

Antonio was looking down at the table when he spoke. I was glad when our number was called because that shit he just said scared me. But at the same time, I felt bad for these guys. They had to do what was neccesary in that situation. They lost a family member to the same shit that Nova was trying to get away from.

He paid for the food and motioned for me to head to the car. I felt protected with him behind me. The ride back to the hospital was a quiet one. The music from the radio was the only sound that was heard. My mind was on the fact that in not so many words, they killed the guy that murdered their cousin. Once we pulled into a parking space at the hospital, he turned the car off and turned to me.

"I know there is a lot going on right now, but I want to get to know you, Monica. You said that you and yo' girls were the only family that Nova has. I'm gonna be the first to tell you that ya'll got us, as well. We ain't going nowhere. That nigga will get dealt with. Don't worry about that. We got ya'll. Now let's go in here because a nigga need to eat," he said with a slight chuckle.

We walked into the waiting room with the bags of food.

"Damn, ya'll was gone for a lil' minute. What the hell were y'all doing?" Scony asked, smirking at Antonio. He was still sitting next to Jade with her head resting on his shoulder. They were a little cozy over there, so I assumed they got to know each other a little bit.

"Nah, fam. It wasn't that kind of party. We went to get something to eat and, yes, I thought about you niggas," he laughed while handing out containers of food.

"Good looking, cuz. I'm hungry as fuck," G said, looking at the doors that lead to the back. "I wish these muthafuckas would come out and give us an update on shorty. I'm tired of sitting here not knowing," he said as he opened the lid to the container of food.

"They will come out soon, I'm sure. Get some of that food in your stomach. Then we can go outside and blow something. That should mellow you out, nigga," said Scony, trying to ease his mind some. I'm glad he was the voice of reason right now.

About an hour later, the doctor came out and informed us that Nova sustained a grazed gunshot wound. They had to shave the left side of her head and applied ten sutures to close it up. We also learned that she lost consciousness because she went into minor shock. He said it's common with people that go through something traumatic. But other than that, he said she would be just fine.

We were allowed to go back and see her for a little while. When I walked in, I was afraid it would be a lot worse than it was. She had a bandage on her head covering the wound and an IV in both arms. They were keeping her hydrated and aministered antibiotics to prevent infection.

She was sleeping, so I took the opportunity to ask the doctor if it was ok if I stayed the night with her. I wasn't leaving my sister there by herself. When I got back to the room, G had moved a chair close to the bed. He just stared at Nova as if she was gonna disappear.

"G, you don't have to worry about her tonight. I'm staying the night with her. Jade, gone on home, but I'll keep you posted. They're about to make you guys leave in a few minutes," I said, explaining the plan while letting out the couch bed on the other side of the room.

"Mo, I'd hate to be the bearer of bad news, but that recliner right there has my name on it." Jade said, pointing to the chair.

"You can always come home with me and I'll bring you back in the morning," Scony said while standing over Jade.

"Nah, my sister comes before anything, hun. I'll have to take a raincheck on that offer. I'm not leaving. Sorry, not sorry," she said, taking her spot for the night.

"I respect that and I understand, but I'm gonna take you up on that raincheck, shorty. When I come to cash in, don't try to act like you don't know what I'm talking about," he said, looking at her lustfully.

I don't know what happened in the short time I was gone, but I'm glad these two met.

"I'll be back later today, Monica. Watch her, okay? Take my number down and call me if there's any changes." G said, walking over to Nova, kissing her on her forehead.

I peeled my eyes away from the interaction between Scony and Jade, giving G my attention. I grabbed my phone out of my purse that was on the couch. I waited for him to finish with Nova. He smoothed her hair down and out of her face, then turned to me. He gave me his number and I programmed it into my phone before I placed it on the nightstand.

"Ya'll drive carefully. See you guys later," I said as I looked at Antonio. He walked over to my phone and picked it up. He tapped away on it and placed it back down.

"Don't hesitate to call me if you need to, beautiful," he said as he hugged me. "Try to get some sleep. She's good now."

"I'll try," was all I could promise him.

Scony said his goodbyes to Jade and they left. I got comfortable on the couch and tried to relax. Jade had already leaned back in the recliner with her eyes closed. I thought about how attentive G was with Nova. He'd just met her and was showing so much compassion for her. I think he's a winner.

Meesha

Chapter 9
Kelvin

"Suck that dick, ma," I moaned while pushing her head deeper into my lap. I was sitting on the couch and this bitch, Laylah, was kneeled in front of me taking this pipe. I hit her up after I left the club and without hesitation she came through.

I thrusted my rod deeper down her throat. This chic right here gave some good ass head. Just watching her spit on my shit and slurp it back up, kept my shit rocked up. She lightly sucked on the tip and stroked my shit with the right rhythm. My toes were curled the fuck up and I felt my nut trying to escape. I couldn't have that shit. I needed to bust in that pussy.

"Get the fuck up and spread them cheeks," I said, slipping on a condom.

Fucking up the vibe we had going, she had to say some stupid shit.

"We've been together six months and you still want to wear condoms, Kels?" she had the nerve to ask with her face twisted up. I looked at this bitch like she had two heads.

"You not that slow, are you, ma? I'm not running up in no bitch raw! For the record, yo' ass been with *me* for six months. Now get the fuck out!" I barked.

I was mad as hell because my shit shrunk down so damn fast. I was looking for that toe curling nut, but this hoe just turned me all the way off.

"But we didn't even f—"

"Bitch, I said get the fuck up and get out! Don't make me repeat myself," I said as I stood up and pulled up my sweatpants.

She realized I was serious, so she got up and put on her clothes. She stood in the middle of the entryway after she was dressed and looked at me with her face twisted up. Then turned and walked towards the door.

"Call me when you get your attitude together," she said.

"Don't wait on that call, ma. You will be blowing me up before you know it," I smirked. "And you bet not slam my muthafuckin' door! In this bitch acting like you my woman and shit. I don't love you hoes. Play ya position and everything will be good," I said, as I walked back to the couch and sat down.

Once she left, I started thinking about what went down earlier tonight. I was out, minding my damn business chillin' with my niggas, Sergio and Red. We were on North Avenue and Hoyne when I got a picture message from Ziva. I opened it up, thinking she was on some freaky shit like she usually was, but that's not what it was at all.

I couldn't believe what the hell I was looking at. It was this bitch, Sabrina—I mean Nova who was all up on some nigga, letting him feel her up and shit. I got heated instantly.

"Aye, nigga, I'm out. I'll catch up with y'all later. I gotta bust a move. Hit me up tomorrow about that business, a'ight?" I dapped my nigga up and walked to my whip.

When I got in the car, I texted Z back and told her I wasn't far from the club. I had to calm myself down because all I saw was red. This bitch thought I was playing with her muthafuckin' ass.

I blazed up a blunt and connected my phone to the bluetooth. I sat there for a hot minute before I pulled off with Juelz Santana's, "My Problem (Jealousy)", blaring through my speakers.

Yeah that's what it's about right? (jealousy yeah)
I never meant to touch you (jealousy Yeah)
Uh, it was the right (jealousy yeah)
I was buggin', high (jealousy yeah)

Whoa, (jealousy yeah)
God forgive me my... (jealousy yeah)
I was wrong as fuck for putting my hands on her, but it was her damn mouth that got her ass rocked that day, I'm not a punk ass nigga. Ain't nan bitch about to talk to me like my veins got pussy running through them. I gave her ample chances to stop talking to me like I'm some bitch made nigga. So, I closed her fuckin' mouth for a couple of months.

I called and went by the house to check on her ass, but she wasn't trying to hear it. It bothered me because I'd been doing her dirty so long, now suddenly it's over? Nah, that's not how this shit works. But I had to show her I wasn't a fuckin' joke.

I pulled up to the club and decided to park down the street and walked back. When I made it to the door there wasn't any security at that muthafucka, so I slid on in unnoticed. I walked through the crowd, looking around to see if I could spot Nova's ass. I didn't see her at first, but once I got close to the middle of the club I saw her looking like she was having the time of her life.

I hadn't seen her smile like that in years. I used to be the only nigga that could have her cheesing in that manner. In my mind I was going ballistic, but on the outside, I appeared calm as fuck. I eased my bitch off my hip. Nobody saw that shit because it was dark as fuck in there. The only light that was on came from the strobe lights.

I couldn't keep walking through that muthafucka like I was there to enjoy the night, partying. I was about to teach this bitch a lesson. Fuck that, the bitch was about to die. I raised my arm and just let my shit ride.

Boc, boc, boc, boc, boc, boc!
I continued to fire until my piece was empty. I turned around and found the closest exist and dipped out. When I got to my car, I sped off like I was a Nascar driver. I placed my

piece in the secret compartment under my radio, then I slowed down and drove like I just got off work. The last thing I needed was to get pulled over.

"I hope I killed that bitch," I said to myself while blazing up.

I felt bad because I really love that woman. She didn't have nobody but me. I used to be her muthafuckin' strength through everything she'd been through. How the fuck she just gon' say fuck a nigga? Oh well, it was over now. I told her not to fuck with me on that bullshit.

I got up from the couch and went to the kitchen to grab the Henny bottle. I needed something strong to take my mind off what I did. One minute my actions were justified, the next minute I'm questioning myself about why I did it. I need to get on one muthafuckin' accord with myself. I didn't have time to be going back and forth about this shit. What was done was done. Fuck it.

I sat down and started rolling up when my phone rang. I let that shit go to voicemail without even looking. It rang two more times before I finally picked it up.

"What up, Z?" I said, sealing my blunt.

"What the fuck is wrong with you, Kelvin? Why the fuck would you come in that muthafucka shooting her like that?"

Ziva was screaming in my ear like I was deaf. I wasn't trying to hear that shit. I guess she forgot she was the one that told me what her twenty was.

"Look, I don't know what the fuck you talkin' about. Get the fuck off my line talking that shit, Z!"

I disconnected the call, grabbed the Henny bottle and turned that muthafucka up, taking a couple long swallows. Blazing up my B, I inhaled and held that shit in before blowing it out. I needed to get bent to get my mind off that bullshit I just pulled out of jealousy.

Chapter 10
Ziva

I knew I should've been heading to the hospital to check on Nova, but this nigga had me fucked up. I was headed to his crib to give him a piece of my mind face to face. I never thought he would go as far as shooting her. He didn't even have to take it there. It bothered me because I didn't even know what condition she was in.

Pulling up to his apartment building, I jumped out and ran up the stairs. When I got to his door, I banged on it like I was the police.

Bam, bam, bam!

Hearing him walk to the door and paused, I knew he was looking through the peephole to see who was at his door. Finally, the locks turned and he opened the door. He stepped to the side, and let me in.

"Why the fuck did you hang up on me, Kels? I didn't send you that message for you to come in that damn club acting like Rambo!"

I stormed into the living room, throwing my purse on the table and grabbed the blunt out of the ashtray. This was right on time. I puffed and held the smoke in my lungs until it burned. I blew it out and did that shit a second time.

"I hung up on your ass because you were spittin' stupid shit over the phone, with your stupid ass. Secondly, you sent that message being messy. So, don't try to act like I just walked in that muthafucka by chance. You did that shit, but now you wanna act like this was my doing."

"I didn't shoot her! Yo' ass did! All I wanted you to do was embarrass her, but you did the most, my nigga. You didn't have to shoot her is all I'm saying. That's my friend—"

"Yo' friend?" he asked, cutting me off. "Shid, I'd hate to be the muthafucka that you don't like. Ain't one muthafucka I know that will do some shit like that to their *friend*.

I jumped up from the couch, throwing the blunt back into the ashtray. I stood in front of him ready to punch his ass.

"I was wrong for getting mad and texting you. I'll admit that, but regardless of what you're saying, she is my friend. I feel bad as hell about what happened to her, so don't act like I don't!"

"You're kidding me, right? You feel bad for her? Did you feel bad when you were fucking me in her bed? Did you feel bad when you were sucking my dick every time the opportunity presented itself? Did you feel bad about knowing that I had a crib that she still don't know about? Get the fuck outta here with that bullshit, shorty. You don't give a fuck about her!" He walked away from me waving his hand.

He then snatched the blunt out of the ashtray and took a swig of the alcohol. The words that he spoke had me thinking about how fucked up my situation was. I've been fucking him for years, but we were never exclusive. We were friends with benefits. I didn't let Nova know that I had slept with him, but I allowed them to get together without uttering a vowel.

Now I'm the reason she was laid up in the hospital. The tears started rolling down my face at rapid speed. I couldn't stop them if I wanted to. I felt like shit, my conscious eating me up on the inside. I went to the kitchen and got a glass, putting a couple of ice cubes in it. I wet a paper towel and cleaned my face, then I walked back into the room that Kelvin was in and poured myself a much needed drink.

"Come here, Z."

Kelvin wasn't even looking my way. He had his head hung low and he was rubbing his head. I just sat there drinking

Henny like it was water. I had to numb the feeling that was tearing me up inside.

"Ziva, come the fuck here, man!" his voice boomed through the room, making me jump a little bit.

I downed the rest of my drink and stood up. My dress had rose all the way up, damn near exposing my ass. I walked over to Kelvin and he hugged my waist.

"Man, I'm sorry for the shit that I said. I don't regret saying it, but you're just as wrong as me, shorty."

He looked up at me with red-rimmed eyes. Yeah, he was high as hell, but he had tears in his shit, too. Kelvin started rubbing the back of my legs. This is not the time for us to have sex. I only came here to get some answers.

He lifted my dress above my ass and went in head first. Parting my lower lips with his fingers, he sucked my pearl into his mouth. I lifted my leg onto his shoulder and I moaned loudly. He rubbed up and down my slit while sucking harder. I grabbed the back of his head and started grinding on his mouth. He stuck two fingers in my treasure pot and his thumb in my ass. I was leaking like a faucet.

"Ooohhhh, shit! Yes, eat that shit, baby. I'm cummin'!" Kelvin continued to suck on my pearl, making me weak with every suckle.

He placed my leg on the floor standing up.

"Face down, ass up," he said as he unbuckled his pants. I did what I was told and the moment I felt his dick at my opening, I came again. Grabbing my waist, he pounded himself into me with a vengeance.

"Shit, this pussy good. This is the reason I can't stop fucking with you, Z. Mmmmmmm, ma, damn!"

I reached back and started massaging his balls and he let out a growl so loud. "Grrrrrrrr, shit! Z, I'm cummin'!"

I fell into the couch and couldn't move. I haven't been fucked like that in a very long time.

"Oh shit! This muthafucka didn't pull out!" I said to myself.

Chapter 11
G

Last night was crazy as hell. When I was viewing the tapes from the club, I wished I could just pause that shit in real time. I zoomed in on the exact moment that Nova got hit and slowed it down. That damn bullet missed hitting her directly by a few inches and went right past my arm.

There wasn't a doubt in my mind that the shooter was her ex. That nigga tried to kill her, but I was gonna get to the bottom of it. The things that Monica told me validated my thoughts. My guys were out watching for this fuck nigga. He better hope he disappeared on his own.

I looked over at the clock and it read seven-thirty in the morning. It was time for me to get up and move around. Throwing the covers back, I walked to the closet and picked out an outfit for the day. On my way to the bathroom, my phone chimed, indicating I had a text message. I picked it up from the end table and opened the message.

Avah: *Good morning, handsome.*

G: *Good morning. What's up?*

Avah: *I was wondering if we could get together today.*

G: *Today won't be good for me. I have some things to do.*

Avah: *I heard about the shooting at the club last night. Are you ok? And who was the bitch that you were all up on all night?*

G: *I don't have time for your bullshit this morning, Avah.*

Avah is a chic that I fucked every now and again. One of her friends must've been at the club last night, then went back and told her what the fuck I was doing. Whoever her reporter was, failed to realize one crucial detail. Avah wasn't my damn woman! For her to open her mouth to question me was blowing the fuck out of me.

She texted back several more times, but I didn't respond to her ass. I guess she figured she would just keep calling until I answered. Her plan didn't work because I didn't have time for the childish shit that she was on. I walked to the bathroom to take care of my hygiene. I brushed my teeth, washed my face, shaved and took a piss before I hopped in the shower. As I was washing my body, my phone continued to ring pissing me off more and more. All I could do was shake my head.

I grabbed a towel and wrapped it around my waist. Picking up my phone, I went into my bedroom and sat on the edge of the bed. I pushed the home button on my iPhone and this nutty ass bitch had called me twenty-seven muthafuckin' times and I had a dozen text messages. *Who does shit like this?*

I got dressed and hit Scony up. The phone rang and he picked up.

"What up, G?" he answered with what sounded like a lung full of that good shit.

"Yo, meet me at the club in an hour. I'm calling an emergency meeting with the crew and all the niggas that was working security last night. I need to know how the fuck this nigga got in my muthafuckin' establishment holding. That shit was never supposed to happen, so that means somebody wasn't on their job, my nigga."

"I feel you on that. Say no more, I'm there. Aye, have you heard anything on shorty?"

"Nah, but I'm gonna swing by there some time today after I take care of this business. I'm heading out go to the club."

"Yep," he said, blowing out smoke.

Disconnecting the call, I went to my messages. I bypassed all the shit Avah was talking about of course. I sent a mass text to everybody on my team.

Me: *EMERGENCY MEETING AT THE CLUB! Be there in an hour and don't be late. Somebody is going to tell me how this punk muthafucka brought that heat in my shit.*

I went to the kitchen to make a quick protein shake, I didn't have time to cook anything. My thoughts instantly went to baby girl. I vibed with her right off the bat and she had me hooked, lined and sinker. The way she carried herself was captivating to me.

I know that we only talked for a short time, but she had high qualities I looked for in a woman. She was breathtakingly beautiful, down to earth and most of all, she was classy. She proved that a woman didn't have to be half naked to be sexy. I liked that. She's the type of woman that would be meeting my mama.

While I was drinking my shake, I figured I'd do a little something to cheer her up at the hospital. I went online and ordered her the biggest edible arrangement they offered. Then I called the flower shop and sent two dozen roses, along with a dozen balloons and a teddy bear. I knew that would make her smile until I got there. I then grabbed my keys and headed to the garage.

***

I pulled up to GSpot, parked in my parking space and got out. I scanned the lot to get an idea of who was already inside. My main hittas were already there. I walked up to the door of the club and as I reached to open the door, I heard a car speeding in the lot. I turned around, pulling my bitch off my hip at the same time, but it wasn't anyone but that stupid bitch, Avah.

How the fuck did she know where the fuck I was? Is this bitch following me?" I asked myself, putting my tool back on my hip.

She jumped out of her car and stormed over to me, talking shit before she got in front me.

"You just gon' ignore me like that, G? I shouldn't have to call you like that and send text messages without a response. That's what we are doing now?"

"First, you can pipe all that shit down when you're talking to me. Secondly, you ain't my woman to be pressing me like you doin', baby girl. The only way you can question what I do or *who* I do is if you were mine. The last time I checked, I was single as a dolla bill." This bitch was pissing me off, but I wasn't trying to go there with her.

"You weren't sayin' that shit the other night when you were fucking me. So why you wanna be poppin' off like you don't give a fuck now?" she said, walking up on me with her finger in my face.

"I don't give a fuck, that's why. The other night we were fuckin', I don't recall having a conversation about anything other than you taking this dick! Don't come for me, shorty, because yo' feelings will be bruised like a muthafucka. Now is there anything else I can do for you, Avah? If not, I got business to attend to."

"Yeah, answer one question for me. Is there someone else in your life?" Her voice dropped a couple octaves.

"It's about to be. Gone about your day, baby girl, and stop following me around this muthafucka."

"Fuck you, G! You ain't shit nigga!" she screamed, swinging on me. She hit me in my face a couple of times, but I restrained myself trying hard to not hit her back. Instead, I turned to go into the club because I don't put my hands on females. But then I realized this bitch punched me hard in the back of my head. I turned around and before I knew it, I yoked her ass up by her throat. I pushed her up against the building so hard, her eyes were big as saucers.

"Don't you ever in your muthafuckin life put your hands on me, bitch! I have killed niggas for far less! Consider yo' dumb ass lucky that you are a female!" I let her go and I left her stupid ass standing there looking dumb as fuck as I walked in the club.

When I stepped through the door I was on ten. Muthafuckas stopped talking to acknowledge me. There were many "what ups" going around. I greeted them back with my head down, took a breather and got down to business.

"I called this meeting because of the shit that popped off here last night. There was minimal damage done, but that shit should've never went down. That's the reason I have security around this muthafucka," I said, looking around. I walked over to the bar and grabbed a bottled water, taking my place back in the center.

"When I viewed the tapes, I looked for specific shit. Bo, yo' azz was ducked the fuck off with some bitch all in ya grill. But I can say this, you were still on ya post observing shit. Everybody was on point except yo' ass!" My voice boomed through the club as I pointed to Von. He stood there like he was about to get gutta at the mouth and I gave him the opportunity. I was hoping his ass didn't try to jump hard. I had been through enough shit and it wasn't even noon. His ass would get fucked up for all of it.

"Man, get the fuck on with that shit! I was where the fuck I was supposed to be. Don't come at me like I'm a pussy muthafucka, man!" he barked.

"So, you telling me that you were at the main door even though I just told yo' punk ass I looked at the tapes, huh? See, you handle my money at the door of the club and you handle my product on the street. How the fuck you expect me to trust yo' ass if you lie in my face, nigga!"

This muthafucka heightened my anger higher than it was when I walked in that bitch. I made it to his ass in three quick strides, I snatched his ass by his collar and punched his ass in the face. He fell over a barstool and jumped back up like he was gon' do something.

"Don't put ya hands on me no mo', G. On the real, dog," he said, wiping the blood from his mouth.

I commenced to whooping his ass like he stole something. First, the nigga wasn't at the door and secondly, I saw his ass skimming off my muthafuckin' money. Then he wanted to puff his muthafuckin chest out like he about that muthafuckin life. I put them paws on that nigga until I got tired. I hit that nigga over every part of his fuckin' body. I tried to paralize that muthafucka. I got off his ass and stood over his punk ass.

"Now, muthafucka, let me tell you why I just fucked you up. You stole from me, bitch ass nigga! Yo' ass wasn't at the door because you were too busy taking yo' cut from my door money, like you weren't getting paid for the night. I don't like a thief, nigga. Get the fuck out before I kill yo' ass! The only reason you're leaving here breathing is because I got respect for your mama. Get the fuck out my shit, Von! You're done, son. I don't need yo' ass around these parts, partna!"

That muthafucka took his time getting up, but when he rose fully to his feet, he had his glock in hand. Before he could raise it, me, Scony and Antonio lit his ass up. It hurted to do that shit, but it was either him or me.

"Take this shit as a lesson and learn from it. Don't bite the hand that feeds you, muthafuckas. We are a family until I find a snake in the grass. Clean this shit up! I'm out. Scony and Tonio, I'm going to the hospital. I'll call y'all later about that other business."

I walked out the club to my ride. I needed to go make sure my future was okay. Besides, I knew seeing her would take my mind off the bullshit in my life.

Meesha

Chapter 12
Nova

When I woke up, I was trying to figure out where I was. Then the events of the night before started flooding back in. I remember having a good time dancing with a fine man named G. He sure knew how to dance. But then I also remembered the sounds of gunshots and the excruciating, burning sensation on the side of my head. The last thing I remembered was G's face before everything went black. I touched the bandage and started crying when I realized my hair had been cut. I thought about everything and thanked God that I was still alive.

I looked over to my right to look out the window and saw Mo laid out on the sofa bed. I then looked around the room and spotted Jade sleeping in the recliner. My heart swelled and fresh tears started to flow. My girls didn't leave me here alone. Ziva must've gone to get breakfast or something because she wasn't here. Usually when you see one, you saw us all.

I picked up my phone, which was plugged up on the nightstand next to the bed to see what time it was. It was after ten in the morning and I was hungry as hell. At that moment, a sharp pain ripped through my head.

"Arrggh!" I screamed out in pain, holding my head. Mo and Jade jumped up simultaneously on alert.

"What's wrong, sis? Are you okay?" Mo asked rushing to my side, while Jade rushed to the other side.

"My head is killing me, y'all. Why do shit keep happening to me? I just don't understand." I broke down crying but that wasn't helping the pain that was overpowering my head.

Mo pushed the call button for the nurse.

"May I help you?" the nurse asked.

"Yes, Nova just woke up and she says her head hurts badly. Would you have someone bring her something for the pain, please?" Mo asked, while she massaged my temple.

"Yes, I will be right in, ma'am."

"Thank you." Mo said.

I calmed down, trying not to think about the things I've been going through, but getting shot was scary. I could have died last night. I was almost one of those people at the wrong place at the wrong time. All this unnecessary shooting was tearing our city apart.

"What are they saying about my condition, y'all?" I didn't know what the hell was going on with myself and I needed to know.

"You were grazed by the bullet, but it left a deep gash on the left side of your head. You had to have ten sutures to close it up. You were unconscious due to minor shock. And they had to give you an IV to administer an antibiotic drip, preventing any infections. Other than that, you will be ok," said Mo, giving me all the information that was relayed to her. I'm glad she was there on my behalf.

Jade was biting her lower lip, looking scared as ever. She hadn't said a word.

"Jade, boo, I'm fine. You don't have to worry about me. Thank y'all so much for staying with me. I really appreciate it," I said, glancing back and forth between the two of them. I opened my arms wide for them to come in for a hug.

"You already knew we weren't leaving your side. That's not how we do shit. We are walking out of here together some time today," Jade said, finally finding her voice now that she knew I was okay.

"Where's Z? She better be out getting some breakfast shit," I laughed, letting both of them go, but I was very serious.

"I'll order you some breakfast. You need something on your stomach before you take those powerful ass meds they're about to bring in here." Mo picked up the phone and ordered me pancakes, eggs, bacon and orange juice.

"We haven't seen Ziva since last night at the club. We don't know where she is," Jade explained.

"Oh my God! Did y'all check to see if she was hurt at the club?" I asked with worry in my voice.

"She wasn't hurt, Nova. She left the club when you were put in the ambulance. We just haven't seen nor heard from here since," Jade said lowly. Mo didn't say anthing for a couple of minutes.

She then went ahead and explained how Ziva was concerned about me while I was laying unconscious until the ambulance came. But I what was trying to figure out was why she wasn't here. I picked up my phone and dialed her number. It rang but she didn't answer. I tried three more times, but all I got was her voicemail. I figured she would call back eventually.

As I placed my phone back down, there was a knock on the door. I thought it was the nurse, but I was wrong. It was someone with a bunch of balloons and a teddy bear. Another person came in with a lot of roses.

"These are for you, Miss LaCour," the delivery man said, placing the flowers on the tables around the room. He then let the balloons float to the ceiling. He retrieved a card from the bouquet he brought along with the teddy bear.. I opened the card and read it out loud.

"I hope you are feeling a little better today. Sending a little something to brighten your day, beautiful. G."

"Awwwwww, that was so sweet! That man got it bad for you, girl!" Jade was more excited than I was. All I could do was smile.

Before I could blink, there was another knock. The first delivery guy left out, while the nurse and someone from the kitchen was coming in.

"You're getting all kinds goodies today, huh, Nova?" the nurse said, smiling. "I have one more for you, as well."

She was holding a big, edible arrangement that had all my favorite fruit dipped in chocolate. It was in a glass container that said, *Get well soon*. There was yet another card attached and I read it just as before.

This should have you smiling brightly until I get there. Get well soon. You owe me a date :) G

"This man is going all out for you, honey. He must be someone special," the nurse stated.

"I don't know. I just met him last night." I was blushing like a schoolgirl. I'd never had a man do anything like this for me before other than my daddy. Kelvin was too busy playing in pussy to do anything special for me.

"Well, I think you need to change that, sweetie. He's a keeper."

The nurse placed my food and meds on the tray in front of me. I offered Mo and Jade some, but they declined and told me to eat.

"Y'all order something for yourselves. I'll give the ok to the kitchen. Miss Nova take those meds after you're done eating. I'm gonna check to see when you will be able to get released. Enjoy your fruit and all of the other gifts as well, hun," the nurse said, looking around in amazement once more before walking out.

All I could do was eat, while thinking about G.

Chapter 13
G

The shit that I had to deal with at the club was really fuckin' with me. Von was a good dude, but he knew he wasn't going to walk out that muthafucka after that. I just don't want to see the hurt that's gonna be on his mama's face when she finds out. But oh well, that was his fuck up.

I was cruising down Michigan Avenue on my way to the hospital, when I happened to look in my rearview mirror. I had to glance twice because I knew muthafuckin' well this bitch wasn't tryin' me. I pulled into the next lane and low and behold, Avah's ass did the same. She watched too many tv shows because she stuck out like a sore thumb behind me. She obviously didn't get the hint back at the club.

I was about five minutes from the hospital and my attitude was fucked up. I had to blow something before my negative vibes rubbed off on my future. She hadn't been with a nigga of my caliber before. Her ex was a fuckin' lame with the shit he pulled last night. That was the only way to describe his ass, but I had plans to show her what being with a grown man was all about.

I pulled into the parking lot of the hospital and blazed up my blunt. I was looking at Avah's wannabe inconspicuous ass in the side mirror. I laughed to myself because this broad was gonna make me choke the life out her stupid ass once again.

Avah was a champion in the sheets, but a birdbrain in the streets. I met her at this Belizean restaurant out south on 63rd street. That ass was everything to a nigga. I was in there picking up some food to go, but decided to sit down and eat with her. We had a decent conversation, but she opened the door about heading to her crib to fuck. That wasn't my doing at all, but I didn't turn that shit down either. After an entire year of me fuckin' her, now she wanted to do the fool.

I finished my blunt and sprayed myself down once I got out the car. I didn't want to go in the hospital smelling like a marijuana plant. Tossing the cologne in the armrest, I grabbed the bag of clothes that I got for Nova. I had to get her some clothes to leave the hospital in because the police took her bloodstained clothes for evidence. Closing the door, I hit the button on my key fob. I made my way to the entrance of the hospital, I didn't even look in Avah's direction. I let her believe she had one up on me.

I walked to the information desk and the broad didn't even acknowledge me when I walked up. She was too busy on the phone holding a whole conversation. I stood there about to curse her ass out, but I kept my composure.

"Excuse me, I'm here to see Nova LaCour in room 720. Would you assist me with a pass, please?" This bitch was acting starstruck and shit, instead of replying to my question. I tried to stay calm but she wasn't making it easy.

"Hello! Would you give me a pass to room 720 for the second time?" I yelled.

"Oh, oh. I'm sorry, one minute," she said, as she typed on the keyboard. "Yes, sorry about that. Here's your pass. Take the elevators on your right, G. I mean, sir," she said, blushing.

All I could do was shake my head. These women knew of me and at the same time, they didn't know shit about me, but was always on a nigga's dick.

"Thank you," I said and walked away.

As I waited for the elevator, all I heard was "Girl, that was G's fine ass! Girl his dick is big ass hell! He had on some grey sweatpants, too. Bitch, yassssss!" She screamed like she was at the bustop and not at work.

The doors to the elevator opened and I got on laughing all the way to the seventh floor.

***

I got off the elevator and every nurse I passed had her eyes on my dick! I had to admit I wasn't an ugly nigga by far. I stood 6'4", about 220lbs, muscled up and skin the color of caramel, but the women fell in love with my green eyes. My daddy was mixed with a little bit of everything, so the eyes came from him.

I couldn't find room 720, so I asked the nurse at the desk. "Excuse me, where is room 720?"

"Ummm, ummmm, sorry. Go down the hall and to your left, sir." she stumbled while blushing and pointing in the direction that she instructed me to go.

"Thank you so much."

I started walking in the direction she pointed. Once again, I heard, "Girl, did you see all of that in them grey sweatpants? That should be against the law for his fine ass. I wonder if he got a woman."

I couldn't do nothing but laugh. These women were a trip.

I stood outside the door and knocked before I entered. When I walked in, the conversation stopped and, once again, all eyes were on me.

"Good afternoon, ladies," I spoke as I walked further into the room, closing the door behind me.

I made my way over to the bed that Nova was sitting up in. She looked much better. Jade and Monica spoke back as I bent down and kissed Nova on the cheek.

"Good afternoon, beautiful. How are you feeling?"

"Hey, G. I'm feeling a little better, I just woke up. Those pain meds knocked me out. Thank you so much for the gifts," she said, turning a deeper shade of red with every second that passed.

"No problem. I couldn't have you sitting in here looking at these hospital walls. This is for you, as well." I handed her the bag that I had in my hand.

"Grant, you have done enough! You didn't have to buy me anything else," she said, looking up at me.

I sat down in the chair so she wouldn't have to strain her little neck. "Everything I've done for you today, I did it because I wanted to. Now look inside the bag, woman," I said, laughing.

She opened the bag and there was a black and grey BeBe shirt, a pair of grey joggers, a pack of underwear, socks and a black sports bra. I didn't know what size bra to get so I took the easy route. There was also a pair of black and grey Air Max, as well. I had her shoes from last night, so I just got that size and asked the salesperson to convert that to a woman's gym shoe size.

"This is too much! And you got me matching your fly. Thank you," she said, laughing.

Jade and Monica were laughing, too.

"G, let me find out you got a thang for my sister," Monica's ass piped in.

"Hey, I'm gonna be here for her every step of the way if she allows me to be. What time are they letting you out of here anyway, beautiful?"

The words weren't out of my mouth a full minute before the nurse came in with the discharge papers.

"Miss Nova, I got your discharge papers." She looked over at me and started blushing with embarrassment. She handed Nova the papers to sign and smiled. "I told you he was a keeper, girl. Don't let him get away."

She collected the papers after Nova signed them, explained what she needed to do as far as wound care and gave her some prescriptions.

"You take care of yourself, young lady, and take care of this gentleman, too. Mmmm, mmmm, mmmm," she said, shaking her head walking out the door.

"What the hell was that all about?" Jade asked.

"Them damn sweatpants! Let me get up and take a shower so we can get out of here," Nova said, getting out of the bed.

Meesha

Chapter 14
Ziva

I rolled over and knew right away that I wasn't in my own damn bed. Looking over, I saw Kelvin knocked out. I cursed under my breath because that wasn't what the hell I came over here for. I came to cuss his ass out for the bullshit he pulled at the club.

I got up and walked over to the chair that I placed my purse in last night. I pulled out my toothbrush and a clean pair of underwear. I decided to go to the car to get my emergency bag once I got out of the shower. Making my way to the bathroom, I grabbed my phone off the dresser. I had many missed calls. When I looked at my call log, I had missed calls from Monica, Jade and Nova. I guess that meant she was alright. I wanted to call them back, but I didn't feel like making up lies about why I wasn't there. I'd figure it out though.

I brushed my teeth and got in the shower. Lathering up my body, my cookie jar was swollen like a muthafucka, Kelvin put in that work last night. I felt guilty as hell sleeping with the man that almost killed my friend. But, shit, I couldn't pass up that dick. I thought back to our sex session and remembered that I needed to go get a Plan B ASAP!

I was rinsing my body when I felt the cold breeze hit my body. Kelvin got in and closed the curtain back. He started rubbing on my ass, but wasn't nothing going down.

"Good morning, Z," he said, as he kissed my neck.

"Good morning, Kels. The shower is all yours," I said. I snatched the towel off the sink and stepped out of the shower. I wrapped the towel around my body and walked out.

"That's how you gon' play me, Z? Do you see what my dick is looking like right now? Stop playing, man!" he screamed.

"I'm not playing. I have moves to make. I'm about to go check on No—I got shit to do." I know how this nigga gets when he hears her name, so I tried to correct that shit. It didn't work though.

"Where is she? Is she still in the hospital? What hospital is she at?" he asked, jumping his ass out of the shower butt naked, dripping water all over the place.

"Would you shut up for a minute? I don't know where she is, but I have an abundance of missed calls from everybody. I'll call to see what's going on when I get home. But Kels, I want you to stay away from her, man." I looked him in his eyes pleading for him to agree.

"I'll stay away under one condition. You find out everything you know about that nigga she was with, I'm killing that muthafucka. He was touching what belongs to me." He turned to walk back into the bathroom to finish his shower, mumbling under his breath.

"Kels, I'm not doing that shit! Leave well enough alone. She really ain't gonna fuck with you once she finds out it was your ass that shot her," I said, slipping on my panties.

He was out of that bathroom faster than Superman himself. He grabbed me by my hair and through clenched teeth he said, "Bitch, you better not tell her shit! Do you understand me? Your ass is just as guilty as I am. I will fuck you up, Z."

I didn't have any plans of telling her shit. His ass was just paranoid.

"Why did you assume that I was gonna tell her anything? I'm just going to check on my friend! Now let my damn hair go, Kels!"

After he let me go, I threw on a pair of his shorts and a tee shirt and walked out to get my bag out of my trunk. When I came back in, he was sitting on the couch smoking a blunt. I walked right past his ass and went to get dressed. I didn't have time for his bullshit. I finished getting dressed in record time, grabbed my shit and was heading for the front door.

"I'm out." I said, without looking at him.

"Nah, you need to let me know that you're gonna find out who that nigga is, Z!"

I was getting tired of him screaming at me like he was my daddy or some shit, he got me fucked up. I did an about face and placed my hand on my hip.

"Kels, this is me you're talking to, not Nova." I let him know, pointing to myself. "I'm gonna need you to lower your tone, my nigga. I already know who the nigga is. I don't have to find out shit."

"Who the fuck is it then, Ziva? Stop playing with me, shorty. That nigga is a dead man walking," he said, hitting the blunt.

"The nigga is G. Are you happy now?" I said, rolling my eyes.

This nigga started choking off the smoke he had just inhaled. Coughing like he was about to die, I ran in the kitchen and got him a bottled water. Rushing back to the living room, I gave him the water and he took a long swallow. After he caught his breath, he was looking at me with a weird look on his face.

"Did you say G? As in Grant Davenport?" he asked with so much excitement in his voice. "This is even better!"

He was jumping around like the Cubs won the World Series again.

"I'm gonna hit this nigga pockets, then I'm gonna kill his ass! Jackpot, baby! It's on now. This nigga messed with the wrong bitch," he said, laughing while pumping his fist in the air.

All I could do was shake my head, leaving him to celebrate whatever stupid shit that was running through his head.

Meesha

Chapter 15
Avah

I had been sitting outside the hospital for over an hour. I was tired of driving, but I had to find out what G was up to. He didn't even know that I'd been trailing him since he left the club. I stayed to follow him because I needed to find out where he lived. That muthafucka choked the wrong one. He was going to get his ass kicked once I told my brothers he put his hands on me. I pulled down the street from the club, so I could still see his car when he left. He thought he was just going to stop fuckin' with me like that and put his hands on me? Nah, that wasn't the way it was going to be with me.

When I met G, I was in a restaurant on the southside. I saw him when he came in and I knew I wasn't going to let him leave without introducing myself. He ended up sitting down, eating his food with me. The man was fine! The way he kept licking his lips made my love box tingle.

I didn't waste anytime getting him to my house. He fucked me so good that night, I was sprung from the first stroke. It's been a year and I still didn't know what those lips feel like. He has never kissed me or my second set of lips, but he didn't have to. He had enough dick to make up for it.

When my girl called me last night and told me his ass was all up in some light-skinned bitch's face, I was on my way to the club. But she hit me back and said they shut the club down because some idiot shot it up. A lot of people got shot, including the bitch he was skinnin' and grinnin' with.

I was listening to K. Michelle's, "Love Em All", when this muthafucka walked out holding this bitch hand. He had a handful of balloons and flowers in his other hand. The female had a teddy bear and a bag in hers. There were two other females with them, as well, but my focus was on his ass. The way he was looking at her had me steaming. He never looked at me like that. To make it worse, the two were damn near matching from head to toe in their black and grey.

They were standing by his car talking. About what, I don't know. But after a while, he put the balloons and shit in the trunk. One of the females handed him an arrangement of fruit and walked off to another car. He walked the bitch to the passenger seat of his Night Black 2017 Benz CLA 250 and had the nerve to open her fuckin' door. I ain't never been outside of my damn house with his ass. He walked to the driver side and got in, and backed out of the parking spot.

I didn't pull right out behind him, but I wasn't too far back. There was a red light, so I took the opportunity to call his phone. I watched this nigga look at his phone and put it back down. That only made me keep calling, but he never picked up.

I followed him until he pulled up to this beautiful home and parked in the driveway. I'd never been to his house, so I didn't know if it was his or hers. I didn't have to speculate too much longer after I saw the two females pulled behind G's car. So, this was the bitch's house. I wrote the address down and pulled the fuck off. She would be seeing me soon.

Chapter 16
Monica

Jade and I were on our way over to Nova's house. We were talking about how G just showed up and showed out for my girl at the hospital. The smile that wouldn't leave her face after she received those deliveries was priceless. I hoped she would give this man a chance, she deserved to be happy. I didn't have an ounce of doubt in my mind that he would hurt her. I believed deep down in my heart that he was the one to love her the way she should be loved.

We pulled up to the house and before I turned into the driveway, I noticed a baby blue Nissan Maxima that was parked on the other side of the street. I didn't get the chance to see who was inside because whoever it was pulled off fast. I wasn't sure if it was Kelvin or not, but I hoped there wasn't any bullshit about to happen. Nova had already been through too much. That was going to be the first thing I inquire about when we got inside.

"Have you ever seen that car that just pulled off, Jade?"

"I wasn't paying attention, Mo. My bad. I was scrolling through the 'Book'. Jade never watched her surroundings, I found myself reminding her of that constantly.

I exited the car waiting on Jade to do the same. I hit the lock button on the key fob and we walked up the steps to the door. Jade rang the doorbell and G answered. He stepped to the side so we could enter. I didn't waste any time asking the question that was buggin' the hell out of me.

"Hey, sis, did y'all see that baby blue Nissan parked across the street when y'all came in?"

Nova looked terrified and shook her head no, then she looked at G. He had an expression on his face that was unreadable. He then pulled his phone out and went toward the kitchen.

"What the hell?" Nova was clueless like the rest of us.

"I'm quite sure he's gonna explain what's going on when he comes back. At least I hope he does," Jade said, sitting on the couch.

"Do you want me to fill your prescriptions or is G gonna do it?" I asked Nova, sitting down on the loveseat as I tried to steer the conversation in a different direction.

"Shit, I forgot to ask him to stop, I just wanted to get home. If you want to go, that's fine. The doctor called them in. All you have to do is pick them up."

"Ok, I can do that. How are you—" I started to ask when G's voice boomed through the house.

"Look, I told yo' ass earlier to stop following me around! It ain't yo' concern what I do. You ain't my woman. Now what I want you to do is find you some muthafuckin' business. This is not the shit you want, Avah! Let this be my last time telling you. If I find out you are coming by this house fucking with her, you're gonna wish you never had!"

We all looked at each other trying to figure out what was going on. When G stepped in the living room, he was rubbing his hand down his face, shaking his head.

"I'm sorry about that y'all. When you described the car, I knew exactly who that was. I feel like I owe y'all an explanation. The person in that car was a woman named Avah. She's someone that I was fuckin' around with from time to time. One of her friends told her that I was socializing with you at the club last night. But when she brought it to me, I shut that shit down. I don't have a woman, Nova. I'm too grown to lie," he said, looking her right in the eyes when he spoke.

"G, I've been through too much and I don't have time for any drama. I don't care what's going on with the two of you, just make sure whatever *it* is don't make it my way. I have my own shit to worry about. Just know I won't hesitate to fuck a bitch up. But it shouldn't be a problem because we are not together," she said, twisting her fingers together.

I stood up and motioned for Jade to follow me. She wasn't getting the hint at all.

"Jade, let's go get Nova's medicine and let them talk," I said, grabbing her arm.

She finally stood and walked with me. "G, please don't be on no crap with my girl. If you're gonna be with her, be with her. She had to deal with a no-good nigga for years. Don't put her through it again," Jade said.

She didn't even give him a chance to respond. She just walked out the house.

Meesha

Chapter 17
G

Avah was one messy ass individual. How the hell she gon' follow me to this woman's house? I was so mad that she did that shit. I hoped she took heed to what the fuck I said. She better let that shit sink into her head. Now here I was, trying to explain myself to Nova. Now she wasn't my woman, but damn, I was trying to get to know her on that level. So, I felt the need to put it all on the table.

I also understood where Jade was coming from, as well. She was protecting her girl, so I couldn't even be mad about her throwing her two cents in. But, my focus was on this beauty that was sitting in front of me.

"I hear what you're saying and I respect that. I'm not here to hurt you, sweetie. When I'm with someone that's just that, I'm with that person. Avah feels that I'm her man because we have been doing what we do for about a year now, but that's all we do. I've never taken her anywhere, she's never been to my house and I've never even kissed her. She knew what it was from the jump. At that time, I told her I wasn't looking for a woman. And I'm still not, a woman found me."

I knew I sound like a soft nigga, but don't get shit misconstrued. I wanted to be able to get to know this woman on every level, without the drama.

"We can take things slow, G. Start off as friends. This woman was before me and I can't do anything about that. But I'm here to let you know, don't try to build something with me while you're still playing fuck games with her. That's all I'm saying. We are not exclusive. This is the beginning," she said, softly with her head down.

I didn't like the way she constantly held her head down. I sat next to her and lifted her head with my fingers under her chin.

"Don't ever let anything in life make you walk around with your head down, you're a gem. I want you to walk with your head held high, no matter what happens. You will never have to hold your head down in my presence. I'm gonna be here with you to build you up, not tear you down. You are beautiful, strong, smart and, most importantly, you are alive. Those attributes alone give you the power to embrace your worth" And I meant every word I said.

She didn't respond. She only nodded her head to let me know she understood. I knew at that point, it was time for me to ask her about her pussy ass ex. I needed to know everything about that nigga.

"There are some things that I need to ask you, sweetie. Don't get mad at your friends because they were just looking out for you."

"I don't know what you're talking about, Grant."

I noticed that she says my whole name when she has a slight attitude, that shit is cute.

"I had some information about the shooting at the club. I looked at the surveillance footage and didn't like what I saw."

"Wait, how did you get access to the footage? You're the police or something?" she asked, looking at me with the look of confusion on her face.

"Nah, baby girl, I'm not the police," I laughed. "I own Gspot, that's my club. I have access to whatever takes place there." Her body relaxed after I explained how I saw the footage.

"This is gonna be hard for you to take in, but I'm here for you every step of the way. I looked at the video several times and that bullet was meant for you, Nova. I couldn't get a good look at the guy because it was dark in the club. Is there anyone that would want to hurt you?"

I waited for her to answer me, but it took a while. I gave her the time she needed and she finally opened up to me. She told me everything that Monica said last night. Listening to her recount of the events pissed me off. I zoned out for a minute, but I caught the tell end of what she was saying.

"I'm sorry. Go back a tad bit because I missed it."

"I was saying that earlier yesterday, he was in my house when I got out of the shower. He choked me and told me that he would kill any nigga that I was with. He left telling me that I belonged to him and I needed to get with the program basically. He has a key to my home, G. He must've duplicated the key that he gave back to me. I need to get my locks changed. I was gonna get them done today, but shit happens, right?" she said, staring off into space as the tears started falling.

I could tell that she was scared because she was visibly shakened. I leaned over and hugged her into my chest until she calmed down. I pulled my phone out of my pocket and hit up my cousin, Antonio.

"Yo, you busy? I need you to come over to Nova's crib and change the locks." He paused for a minute.

"Hold on, let me ask. Nova, how many locks need to be changed?" I asked her.

"There's three on the house, but I want the garage door opener changed and the lock on the shed."

I repeated everything back to Antonio.

"Ok, cool. I'll text you the address. Bring Scony with you, too. I have some information for y'all. Yep, bet." I disconnected the call, looking down at her as she continued to cry.

"What's wrong, sweetie?" Every time she cried, my heartstrings pull tight.

"My head is killing me. I think I need to lay down. I'm gonna call Mo to see what's taking them so long."

She dialed Monica's number and I took the phone from her hand, resting her head on my chest.

"Yeah, boo. Are you ok?" she asked as soon as she answered.

"She's ok, Monica. Her head is hurting. Were you able to get her meds?"

"Yes, we're right down the street. Tell her I'll be there soon."

"Ok, bet," I said, laying the phone on the table. I looked at her head and saw that her bandage needed to be change.

"I'm gonna go to the car and grab your things. Your bandage needs to be changed."

She nodded her head and closed her eyes. I held her head and eased from under her, placing her head on the couch pillow. I stood up looking at her then turned to go to the car.

It didn't take me long to grab everything. As I closed the car door, Monica pulled up. I waited for them to get out. I loved the bond that these ladies had for each other and Monica and Jade thought of everything with pizza and Chinese food in hand, I didn't even think to ask Nova if she was hungry.

I met them halfway and took the pizza boxes from Monica. We walked the short distance to the house and the two of them climbed the stairs. Before my foot could hit the first step, I heard Antonio's music bumping. I shook my head because that nigga was going to be deaf before he is forty.

"Who is that?" Monica asked, turning around.

"That's Scony and Antonio. We got some business to discuss and Antonio is gonna change the locks in the house." I explained, but it went on deaf ears because they both were staring my niggas down like they were a fresh glass of water.

Chapter 18
Antonio

When I pulled up to the address G sent me, the first thing I saw was Monica's thick ass. I had been thinking about that woman since I left the hospital. When G called and told me what was up, I knew she would be here, as well.

I loved a chocolate woman who wasn't ashamed of the curves that she carried. Baby girl walked with so much confidence and with her head held high. That's the shit I talked about all the time, the confidence that a woman should have in herself. She was a woman that didn't care about what anyone else thought about her. Monica stared at my car like she wanted somebody to be on some bullshit. When me and Scony got out the car, I could see her eyes light up and a small smile appeared on her face.

"Hey Antonio, Scony," Monica waved.

"Hello, gorgeous." Antonio said.

"Hey Mo," Scony replied with a head nod.

We were staring each other down as I walked up to G.

"What up, nigga?" G asked, giving me a half hug. He did the same with Scony.

"Ain't shit shakin', I just wanted to come on through and get baby girl situated like you asked. Man, what's the word on this nigga? What info you got for us?"

"Well, Nova don't know where this nigga is laying his head, but she knows where his mom and sister live. He was working at the University of Chicago Hospital on Cottage Grove. He drives a smokey grey, 2016 Chrysler 300 license plate number 687239, and his birthdate is April 7, 1988. Once I told her that nigga was the person that may have shot her, she ran his background with minimum hesitations." G said, relaying the information that Nova gave to him.

"That's useful information, brah. I will pass that along to Quan and get shit shakin'," Scony said as he took his phone from his hip, and shot Quan a text. He was always on top of the business, that was one of the reasons G chose him as his right hand.

"Let's go inside before this pizza gets cold. That will give the ladies a reason to argue. I gotta tell you niggas what that bitch, Avah, did too," G said, climbing the stairs.

"Don't tell me she on that goofball ass shit, brah," Scony said, climbing the stairs behind me.

"Hell yeah, she is, nigga. Bitch had me acting out of character earlier at the club," G said, pausing at the door. He started telling us what happened and I couldn't stop laughing. The shit was funny.

"Damn, G. I can't believe she punched yo' ass. There's niggas out in these streets that wouldn't even attempt that shit. That's why yo' ass came in the club on a hunnid. Von took that ass whoopin' that yo' ass couldn't give her," I said, laughing.

"Man, ya'll know I don't put my hands on any female. That bitch made me choke the fuck out of her dumb ass. But that didn't stop her crazy ass from following me from the hospital to here. I called that bitch and cussed her ass out. I hope she heard the words I spoke because I won't hesitate to get one of my cousins to whoop her ass."

"Say the word, nigga. I don't give a fuck if she is a female. If she is hittin' a muthafucka, she can be touched. Her mammy should've taught her to keep her muthafuckin' hands to herself," Scony said seriously.

"Scony, I'm not giving you the okay to fuck that bitch up. Calm yo' ass down, nigga," G laughed as he turned the knob and walked into the house.

As we came through the door, I could hear the ladies talking and giggling. Once we entered the living room, we could hear a rat piss on cotton. That's how quiet it had gotten.

"Hello, Nova. How are you feeling?" I asked with a smile on my face.

"I'm fine thanks for asking and you are?" she asked, sitting up from the couch she was laying on.

"I'm Antonio, G's cousin. I forgot we didn't get a chance to meet, but I feel like I know you already. This is Scony. He's family, as well," I said, pointing to Scony who was still standing at the door.

"Hey, Nova. Nice to finally put a voice to such a beautiful woman. I'm glad you are feeling better," he said smoothly. G was going to beat his ass flirting with his woman.

G was in the kitchen putting the pizza away. He walked back to the living room and sat down beside Nova, pulling her close kissing her forehead.

"Scony, didn't I tell yo' ass she was off limits, lil' nigga?" G said playfully. Nova hit him on his arm. That made all of us laugh.

"Man, I don't want no problems." Scony threw his hands up, walking over to Jade kissing her cheek.

"I got one I'm trying to get know. Ain't that right, Jade?" he said, tweaking her nose before he lifted her up and sat her in his lap. She started blushing and hid her face in his arm.

I took a seat on the loveseat where Monica was, but she wanted to act like she was shy and shit. I noticed that Nova kept squinting and holding her head. The gash that she received last night was bleeding a little bit.

"Hey, Miss Nova. You good over there?" I asked with concern.

"Yeah, my head hurts a little bit, but I'm fine," she said, leaning her head on G's shoulder.

"Do you want Chinese or pizza, ma?" he asked her.

"I'm not too hungry."

"You have to eat something before you take your meds. I have to change the dressing on your head, too," G sternly said to her while rubbing her shoulder.

He didn't wait for her to say what she wanted to eat, He got up and went to the kitchen. When he came back, he had a plate of Chinese rice and an egg roll for her to eat. Then this nigga sat down prepared to feed her like a baby. It had been a while since I'd seen him act this way with a woman.

"I can feed myself, Grant. Thanks anyway," she said, laughing.

"Girl, you better let that man take care of you. We ain't gonna always be here. I'm trying to get one of them like you," Monica said. Both her and Jade started laughing.

"I'm not gonna lie and say I'll be trying to feed ya ass, but I know when I sink my claws in yo' pretty ass, yo' ass ain't goin' no damn where," Scony crazy ass said, rubbing on Jade's thigh.

"I guess that's my cue to start on these locks."

I pushed up off the loveseat and went to the door to get my equipment. I had that feeling that someone was watching me as I bent over. I turned around and sure enough, I caught Monica who didn't turn around fast enough. I then decided to fuck with her a little bit.

"Hey, love. You wanna help me change these locks?" I smirked and winked at her. If she wasn't so dark skinned, her cheeks would be burning red.

"I don't know nothing about changing locks, I'm about to get something to eat anyway." She stood up and put her hands on her hips.

"Shid, I'm hungry, too. You gon' feed a nigga?"

I looked her up and down licking my lips. Scony and G bursted out laughing. I don't know what they were laughing for. I wasn't joking at all.

"Do you want Chinese or pizza? That's about all I can help you with right now." she said, trying to hide the smile that was creeping to her lips.

"I'll take pizza with a side of you for dessert," I said, taking the tools I would need out of the bag.

Meesha

Chapter 19
Kelvin

I was doing about eighty-five on the Eisenhower Expressway, happier than a kid in a candy store. When Ziva told me who the nigga was that Nova was all over, I knew that I had to formulate a plan. G was one nigga that didn't take shit lightly when you came at him. I had to get some reinforcement on my side and there was nobody else out there but my nigga, Sergio. Sergio couldn't stand G's ass, and had been waiting on the opportunity to jack him.

I hit him up earlier and told him that I was coming through. See, Sergio was doing his own thing on the westside. He was small time, but we were about to hit these niggas to widen shit up. I pulled up to his crib on Division & Christiana and there were all kinds of muthafuckas outside. This is the only thing I hated about this nigga, he had too much activity at his spot.

I got out the ride and Sergio walked up with his pants hung low with a wife beater and Tims on. It's hotter than a muthafucka out here even though it was September, and this nigga got on boots. But I knew he stayed ready to stomp a nigga's ears together.

"What up, homie? What's good wit' ya?" he asked, dappin' me up.

"Not shit, really. Aye, sit in the whip with me so I can tell you what it is." I walked around to the driver side while Sergio got in on the passenger side. Once the doors closed, he fired up that loud. He took a couple of hits and passed that shit.

"So that nigga G is on my hit list. He done violated like a muthafucka and I'm gonna hit his muthafuckin' pockets. Then I'm gonna kill him." I hit the blunt and passed it back to him. "His ass don't know what the hell he just involved himself in."

"I can't stand that nigga, man! I don't give a fuck what he did, I'm in on whateva. He thinks he's big shit around these muthafuckin' streets. It's time for somebody to knock him down a notch. It may as well be us. I ain't jacked a nigga in a minute, Shid, I'm ready," he said, rubbing his hands together.

We were going over ideas of how to get at this nigga when my phone started ringing. I pulled it off my hip and it was Ziva.

"What up, Z?" I paused to hear her out. She sounded mad, but the information she gave me pissed me off instantly.

"That nigga at her crib? Yeah, a'ight. Good looking. Don't even go in that muthafuckin' house. I'm about to go through that bitch. Take yo' ass home." I disconnected the line and looked at Sergio.

"Do you have some shooters out here right now? I need to roll. This nigga done fucked up."

"Yeah I got you, fam. When you want to roll?"

"Right muthafuckin' now. This nigga gon' wish he never met that bitch." I spat.

***

Sergio gathered two of his best shooters and the four of us rolled out. Nova lived on the near northside, so it took us about twenty minutes to get to her neighborhood. I left my car parked by Sergio's crib and hopped in this lil' hooptie with them. I checked my .380 and my nine mil, I wasn't about to play with these muthafuckas. Sergio had the AK47 in his lap ready. I didn't know what the other lil' niggas had, but I knew we were locked and loaded.

"Kels, ain't no babies in this damn house, is it?" the nigga, Pat, asked.

"Nah, ain't no babies or old people in there, but there are some bitches in that muthafucka. They better learn how to duck today. Right about now I don't give a fuck. They should know who the fuck they're laying up with. Let's do this," I said, gripping my guns.

We eased up the street and got to the house. It was still a little early, but I didn't give a fuck. I had to handle this shit and wasn't no better time than now. We jumped out and just lit the house up. We didn't give a fuck if we hit anyone or not. I was sending a message that I'm not bullshitting with this bitch. The windows exploded with every bullet that hit them. The door was riddled with bullet holes and so was the garage. I knew this nigga drove a Benz. That muthafucka was pretty, too. I directed my shots right at that muthafucka and didn't let up until I was empty.

"What the fuck! You gots to be kidding me!"

I emptied two clips in that nigga's car and there wasn't a scratch on it. This muthafucka had the entire car bulletproof. Them niggas came from around the side of the house, busting back. Pedro got hit in the back and he wasn't moving.

"Come on, nigga. Let's go!" Sergio said, jumping in the car.

We all got in and Pat peeled out. I looked out the rear window and I saw them niggas standing over Pedro's body. They won't find nothing on him because he didn't have no identification on him. Pat rounded the corner and we were headed back to the westside. That was only the beginning of what's to come for them bitches.

Meesha

Chapter 20
Ziva

It's been damn near twenty-four hours since I talked to any of the girls. I listened to the voicemails and read the text messages that Nova sent me, but hadn't returned any of that shit, but I planned on hitting her up once I left the salon. I was getting my faux locs redone, I could never be seen out here looking like a basic bitch.

I was thumbing through my phone when this bitch that was waiting, started talking loud as fuck to somebody on her phone. I could be ratchet at times, but I would never put my business out there for everybody and their mama to talk about. I couldn't stand that shit. I rolled my eyes and focused back on my phone. I had my earbuds in and it was about time that I tuned this chic out.

"Girl, you just don't know how bad I wanted to get out that car and beat that bitch ass. He bought her all kinds of balloons, flowers, edible arrangements and shit. Mmhmm. They were even dressed alike down to the shoes, bitch! Well, not exactly, but the same colors."

This broad didn't have no shame at all. She sat there letting everybody know that she was big mad over some shit a nigga was doing for another female. She sounded goofy, straight up.

"Look, G better stop fucking with me. That's all the fuck I know. He ain't gon' just stop fucking with the kid, it ain't that easy. I will turn his world upside down," she spat.

Now she had my undivided attention. I was all ears at that point. I didn't even attempt to find any music on my phone to occupy my time. She saw him with another bitch and she is salty as fuck. I couldn't do nothing but laugh to myself, but my kitty got moist from the words she said next.

"He just don't know that I've followed him enough to know where all his traps are. Bitch, I will have some niggas run through them muthafuckas, air them out, then strip them of everything! Ain't nothing like a woman scorned, he better ask somebody about me."

I sat there trying to figure out how I could start a conversation with her. I had to befriend this bitch quick and get her to see that G was all about Nova. With this bitch knowing what she knows, I had my inside connection to lots of dope and money.

I was under the dryer and my ass dozed off for a minute. When ole girl finished her conversation, I basically knew that she was just a fuck buddy that wanted to be more. I looked to my left and low and behold, the broad was sitting next to me. She had gotten her nails done, so that's how I sparked up a conversation.

"Girl, your nails are cute! Let me see them, who did them?" I asked, acting like I cared about her nails.

"Shay did them, girl. She always does a nice job on my nails," she said, pointing to the nail tech in the corner.

"Oh, ok. That's what's up. I'm gonna have to come in and let her do mine." I was still pretending to admire her nails.

I started playing with my phone, making my ringtone sound I acted like someone called.

"Hello. Yeah, I'm at the salon getting my hair done. What happened? Nova got shot? When? Nah, I didn't know. Me and her ain't cool no more, so I don't know shit about her life. I feel bad about her getting shot but…" I paused like I was listening. "What you say now? Grant Davenport? Hell naw, bitch! How did she pull that shit off?"

I saw baby girl sit up and act like she wasn't listening, but I already knew the truth. I was laughing my ass off on the inside, I had to drag it on a little longer.

"She wouldn't know what to do with a man like him. Don't he got a woman or some shit? I don't know. Hell, that's why I asked. Girl, I'm being rude. I was talking to someone before you called. I'll hit you up when I leave. A'ight, later." I pretended that I disconnected the call.

I didn't know for sure, but I think she was waiting for me to say something, but I didn't. I knew it wasn't going take long for curiosity to get the best of her.

"Excuse me, I'm Avah. I didn't mean to listen in on your conversation, but do you know G?" she asked, turning toward me.

"Nah, I don't know him, but I know of him. I'll let you in on my conversation so you won't have to ponder. One of my associates were calling to give me some news about someone that I used to be friends with. She got shot last night at GSpot and she informed me that G has been by her side since everything went down. But I don't care who she is spending time with to be honest. We don't rock like that no more." I waited for her to continue probing.

"Well, that's good that you don't fuck with her because I'm gonna have to beat her ass about my man. I don't play that shit." She rolled her eyes with the ugliest scowl I'd ever seen on a female.

I had to play her game to get in good with her. So, I said what I thought she wanted to hear.

"Shid, I'll give you the bitch address. Go knock on the door and beat her ass up. Somebody needs to whoop her ass, she thinks she's all that."

I was egging this bitch on to get the brakes beat off her ass. Nova was soft spoken and mild mannered, but she knew how to throw them hands with the best of them. We did a lot of fighting because of jealous hoes when we were younger.

"I got the bitch address. I followed his stupid ass over there today. I'll be visiting her soon enough. He called me earlier trying to check me and told me I better not come back to her house. He may as well have been talking to a brick wall because I wasn't listening. But her day is coming, believe that."

"I have one question though. Why are you so mad at her? I mean she just met him last night. Why aren't you directing your anger at him? He's the one that lays down with you, not her. She may not even know about you. Did you think about that? If that's gonna make you feel better, fuck her up, but that still leaves the deception of your man up for discussion."

"You are right and I like your bluntness. Girl, take my number down. I'd love to kick with you. You seem cool as hell."

I put her number in my phone and texted her so she could have my number, as well. At that precise moment, Keyla, my stylist, came and checked to see if my hair was dry. It was, I paid her and gathered my things to leave.

"I'll hit you up soon, but don't let nobody make you look stupid out in these streets. You can't hold on to a man that don't want to be kept, keep that in mind. It was nice meeting you, Avah. I'm Ziva, by the way. Lock me in, boo."

I walked out of the salon to my car, I got in and decided that I was gonna go see Nova.

***

I took the ride to Nova's house and decided to call her to let her know that I was on my way over. I dialed her phone and it rang a couple of times, then it was answered.

"Hello."

I had to look to see if I dialed the right number. She never let anyone answer her phone.

"Hello," the guy said again. I cleared my throat and decided to respond.

"Hello, may I speak to Nova?" I asked, nicely.

"Nova is sleeping right now. Can I take a message?" he asked before I heard Mo in the background asking for the phone.

He obviously handed her the phone because she started talking.

"Z, where the hell have you been? We have been calling you since last night and why the hell didn't you come to the hospital? This is supposed to be your best friend that got shot! Not one time did you even attempt to check on her! The dick was that important that you saw her laying on that floor bleeding from her head and you weren't the least bit concerned?" Mo had so much venom dripping from her lip, but I didn't care.

"Who do you think you are raising your muthafuckin' voice at? I'm not a damn child. You better watch your tone. Something came up, so I didn't make it to the hospital. I was on my way there now, but I'm not coming because I'll slap the fuck out of you on sight. Just tell Nova that I'll talk to her later." I hung up on that bitch. She got me fucked up.

I parked down the street to cussed Mo's ass out. When I looked towards the house, I saw her standing outside with G, Jade and two other niggas. I assumed she was telling them about the conversation because she was waving her hands around and twisting her neck. I had something for them. This friendship been over anyway. Fuck them.

I dialed Kelvin's number and he picked up. I let him know that I was over Nova's house and G and some other niggas was there along with Mo and Jade. He was mad as fuck and I knew he was about to be on dummy. He told me not to go in the house and to go home. Shid, his crazy ass didn't have to tell me twice. I drove the fuck off once I saw them go back in the house.

Chapter 21
Scony

Jade is one cool female. We hit it off good just on the friend tip. See, I'm a man that has had many women. I have only been in love once and that female tore my heart apart. Never again will a woman get that close to me again, but laughing with Nova's homegirls was something I haven't done in awhile. These chicks were funny and they loved the hell out of their girl.

They had been there for her from the start of this nightmare that she was enduring. Nova went to sleep and woke up screaming, reliving the bullshit that happened to her. She had a great support system of two and three more when you added us. My nigga is really feeling her after damn near twenty-four hours. Anytime he heard her move, he stopped what he was doing to check on her. He's changing bandages, fixing plates and shit, and handing out medicine. He didn't do that shit for anyone but his grandma before she passed and his mama.

We were all in the same boat with these women out in these streets, fuck 'em and leave 'em. But we haven't tried to get close like that with any of these ladies. Antonio hinted around jokingly, but he ain't trying to go there yet. When Monica went outside to talk to whomever was on the phone, we could hear her hollering all the way inside the house. Tonio was the first one to check on her. We had to be on point about everything until we found out where this nigga Kelvin was. Nova gave us some very important information and we had several spots being watched as we spoke.

Monica was saying something about the person being her best friend, but shit I thought it was only her and Jade. No wonder she was upset. There was a fourth person in their crew that hadn't showed her face at all. I do remember a female at the club, but I wasn't paying attention to her.

But I don't care what the hell came up, she should've deadened that shit from jump. She didn't know if her girl was seriously injured or not. I think we need some information on her, as well, because shit ain't smellin' right with her either. Monica finally hung up the phone. She looked like she was about to cry.

"Who was that, Mo?" Jade asked with attitude.

"That was that bitch, Ziva, talking about something came up and that's the reason she wasn't with us at the hospital. She can miss me with that bullshit. When I see her, I'm fuckin' her up. No bullshit."

Her nostrils were flared out like a bull that was about to charge.

"As much shit as Nova have done for her inconsiderate ass, she should've been the first one by her side. Something ain't right. I feel like she had something to do with all this shit. She has been acting funny and distancing herself from us since Nova and that bastard split. Time will tell though."

"You don't have to worry about it because if you don't catch her, I will. I'm done with her, she's been talking slick at the lip for too muthafuckin' long anyway. I told Nova a long time ago to stop fuckin with her. She's hiding something, Mo. I just don't know what it is. I agree with what you are saying," Jade said, shaking her head and biting her lip.

"Let's go back inside. I'm getting a bad feeling standing out here. I'm gonna need everything y'all know about y'all friend," Antonio said as he looked around with his hand on his hip, making sure his girlfriend was in place.

"I wish a muthafucka would! That would be the last time they pull up. Believe that shit!" G said, scoping out the block, as well.

We all went back into the house and went straight to the living room. G went to check on baby girl. I sat next to Jade and she started telling me what I needed to know about Ziva. Monica and Tonio was listening and chiming in, as needed. Ziva sounded like she was a jealous friend to me, but I didn't think she would go as far as setting up Nova. We couldn't rule anyone out though. We had to keep trying to put the puzzle together.

"We are gonna find out what the deal is sooner than later. There's no telling if this nigga—"

My words were cut off when the windows shattered. G came crawling out of the bedroom with his gun in hand, but he would have been a stupid muthafucka to try to go outside.

"I know muthafuckin well this nigga ain't this stupid," G spat, checking his other gun.

There were so many bullets ricocheting off walls, glass flying all over the front of the house. Whoever the fuck was bustin' at this house didn't come to play. They came to kill. G crawled back to the bedroom to see if they were shooting on that side of the house, as well. They weren't, so he hollered for us to come back there.

He placed Nova on the floor with her head in his lap when a bullet hit the bedroom wall right above the headboard. I crawled back to the front of the house. These niggas were running out of ammo. If I didn't hear that damn AK47 going off, I was going. Antonio and G was right beside me.

"We are about to go out the side door! Blast anything moving! These muthafuckas have to die!" G said as he moved to the door with caution.

We went out the side door and around to the front of the house bustin' at them niggas, catching them off guard. G got one of them niggas in his back. The other three niggas jumped in an old school Chevy and peeled off. Them niggas were pussy muthafuckas. You never left one of ya own. I don't give a fuck what happens.

"I got a partial plate number, my nigga. That was an old ass Chevy, about an 88'. It won't be long before we track it down," Scony said.

We walked over to the dude laying on the sidewalk, but he wasn't gonna help with shit. G shot his ass in the back and it went through his chest. He was a Latino nigga, but we will find out soon who he is.

"Call the cleanup crew. This nigga just started a war," G said, going to check on the ladies.

Chapter 22
Nova

The police were all over my house. It took them damn near twenty minutes to get here, which was good because it gave G and his crew time to get the unknown guy from in front of my house. They cleaned up the blood and everything. I was asked so many questions that my head started to ache.

"Can she please contact y'all later? I mean she's not up for all of this right now," Mo said to the police.

"We are trying to get to the bottom of things, ma'am, and we are doing our job," the officer said with too much attitude.

"If you were trying to do your job, it wouldn't have taken y'all twenty minutes to get here. We were lucky that no one was injured. Now she gave y'all a statement and that's all she got for you," G said, standing up.

The officers looked at G and thought better than to say something slick. With all the police brutality going on, I was scared.

"I will call the precinct once I secure my home properly. I'll make sure to do that tomorrow," I reassured the officers.

They all started filing out and the guys that Scony called were already boarding up the windows on my house. I guess I'll be going to Mo's house. Why is this shit happening to me? That has been the question of my life lately.

***

It's been a month since all the life changing events happened to me. I took off work for six months, putting in for short term disability after the incident with my jaw. Then I was shot, I had to heal properly and needed time to do so. On top of that, now I must figure out what I was gonna do about my home. It had been fixed up for a couple weeks now, but I refused to go back.

I'd been camping out with Mo, but I had also been spending a lot of time with G. That gave us the opportunity to get to get to know each other on a different level and I'm feeling him. He listened to me, made sure I was doing alright and he looked after me. We were always going out somewhere and I enjoyed it. It was sure to be an eventful night if it was one of the triple date nights with Antonio, Mo, Scony and Jade. We had all became close that it felt like we were family.

"Nova! Where you at girl?" Mo had just got off work. She barged in this house screaming my name like that everyday. I'm so glad my headaches are gone completely, because if they weren't, I would never have been taken off those pain pills with her around.

"I'm in the guest room," I screamed back. Mo popped her head in, smiling from ear to ear.

"You can stop smiling. Why do you have to scream through this house like a mad man every day? It doesn't make any sense at all," I said, rolling my eyes at her.

"I have to keep you on your toes. Hey, it's October! All the Halloween festivities are starting, so let's go out and have some fun. How about we go to the Statesville Haunted Prison?" she suggested.

"Now you know damn well I don't like to be scared under no circumstance, you tried it though," I laughed nervously.

"Come on, sis, live a little, please." I hated when she got to begging and pleading, but I would have to think about this one.

"I'll think about it, but I'm not making any promises though." Then my phone chimes, indicating I had a text message.

G: *Hey, gorgeous. How u doin?*

Me: *I'm fine and yourself?*

G: *I can't complain. Can I see u tonight?*

Me: *Sure.*

G: *I'll be thru about 8. See u later.*

"That man can make you smile at any given time. I don't care what mood you're in, he's gonna make it a happy one."

"Hush, chile. He's coming to take me out tonight. I'm not gonna lie Mo, I really like him. I'm just scared to open my heart to him."

I was speaking truthfully. I had been through so much, but I didn't want to let a good thing pass me by.

"You can't let the things that happened stop you from living your life, sis. You will never be happy if you allow doubt to set in. Go with the flow, stop thinking about it. In my honest opinion, G has proven that he is all about you, sis. He is giving you the time you need to decide what direction you want to take what ya'll have. I like that he is not pressuring you about this, but he's still there for you."

"That's exactly what I'll do, go with the flow. G has been very patient and I am very grateful for the things that he does to keep my mind off my situation. I have been fighting the feelings that I have for him. I just don't want to get hurt." I paused for a moment, sitting on the edge of the bed.

"I've been thinking about something for quite sometime now, Mo. I'm going off the subject, but is it just me, or do you think Ziva had something to do with the shooting at my house last month?"

I had to ask because it's been in the back of my mind since I heard she called that day. I hadn't seen nor talked to her since the shooting at the club. Then she and Mo had words and my house got riddled with bullets. It didn't sit well with me at all.

"I've thought about it several times, but I refuse to dwell on it because the truth will come out. I'm just worried that we haven't heard anything from her or Kelvin. The silence is killing me. I think he has sat back for an entire month and has something up his sleeve. G has your back, so I'm not worried about anything and you shouldn't either. Now let's find you something to wear on this date. We are packing you an overnight bag, too. Those cobwebs need to be cleaned out," she laughed, while rambling through my closet.

"That's not funny, Mo. Ain't nobody but your ass thinking about having sex. You need to call Antonio up and stop trying to live vicariously through me," I shot back.

Chapter 23
G

I pulled up to Monica's house with a dozen roses. I was smelling good, haircut was on point, facial just right and I was dressed to impressed. I had on a collarless black shirt, with baggy black jeans and I threw on my red and black low top Jordans. I reached out and rang the doorbell. I propped my shoulder against the doorframe when I heard someone approaching the door. When it opened, I instantly smiled. My future looked sexy as hell. She had on a black, off the shoulder blouse, black skinny jeans and a pair of red 'fuck me' pumps.

"Hello, beautiful. You're looking good tonight. I see you like matching my fly. These are for you," I laughed, handing her the roses.

"Thank you so much. I guess great minds think alike. Let me put these in some water and we can get out of here," she said, blushing.

Before she could turn around, Monica was right there taking the flowers from her hand. "I got these for you and you forgot this." She handed her a bag of some sort.

"Really, Mo? You are something else," she said, laughing.

"Let's go before I have to hurt this woman, G. I'll talk to you later, critter," she shot back at Mo.

"Don't do nothing I wouldn't do," Mo laughed and slammed the door.

I helped Nova into the car and closed the door. Walking to the driver side, I saw her follow me the entire way with her eyes. I opened the door and got in. I turned and winked at her just to see her blush.

"Did you like the view, Miss Nova?" I smiled at her and her face turned three shades of red.

"Boy, stop playing and drive this car. What are your plans for tonight?" she asked.

"I'm all man over here, but I'll save that for another day. I would hate to have you pass out on me and I'll have to do mouth to mouth on you. I thought we would go enjoy dinner and a movie at the IMAX theater. I figured we would go see *IT*." I took my eyes off the road to see her reaction.

"Grant, I hate scary movies. If you didn't notice, I sleep alone. And I was scared watching that damn movie back in the day."

"Well, I'll be there to protect you every step of the way. You can use my chest as your shield when the killing occurs," I laughed.

She raised her hand and traced the dimple in my cheek. I reached up and grabbed her hand, kissing and holding on to it. I hadn't felt this way about a woman in a long time. I felt like Nova could be Mrs. Davenport one day. I just had to break that wall down that she had up. That muthafucka was built like Fort Knox. I am a fighter, and I'm gonna get to the heart behind the wall.

* * *

The movie was great and, yes, she was scared as hell. It wasn't scary to me, but you know women. I decided to take her on a carriage ride along Michigan Avenue. She had never been on one before so she was very excited. We caught the last one of the night.

"I've never looked at the city in this way before. Thank you for experiencing this with me," she said, laying her head on my shoulder.

"I'll do whatever it takes for you to open up your heart to me, Nova. I have great plans for us, I'll wait as long as it takes." There I go acting like a soft nigga again.

When the ride ended, we walked to the car hand in hand. It was getting kind of chilly, so I wrapped my arm around her shoulders rubbing her arm to try to keep her warm.

"I really enjoyed myself tonight, G. I haven't had a good intimate night out in a very long time. I don't want the night to end," she said, looking up at me.

"What did you have in mind, Miss Nova?"

"I was thinking maybe I'd stay the night with you, if that's okay."

"That's fine with me. I have a question for you though. When will you return to your home? I had it fixed up weeks ago, but you still haven't attempted to go home." I glanced down at her and she was looking straight ahead.

We reached my car and I opened the door for her. I waited until she was comfortable and closed it. I didn't let the question go unanswered when I got in.

"I'm waiting on your response, babe," I said, starting the car.

"I think I want to sell the house, G. I can't go back there. There's too many bad memories there for me. I'm gonna look for a condo or something, but in the meantime, I think I'm just gonna sell it."

"There isn't anything wrong with that and I understand. If there's anything I can do to help, let me know."

"You have been of great help in the past month and a half, and I appreciate it." She was staring out the window with a look of concern on her face.

"What's on your mind, love? Talk to me."

"It's nothing. I'll talk about it soon, just not tonight." She laid her head against the window and closed her eyes.

Meesha

Chapter 24
Nova

I woke up to G whispering my name in my ear, kissing me on my cheek repeatedly. I stretched a little bit and turned my head towards him. Our lips connected and his lips felt just as soft as I imagined they would. My eyes closed instantly and I deepened the kiss. I opened my eyes when I felt him pull back. I reached over and wiped the lipstick from his lips.

"Let me get you inside so you can get some sleep beautiful," he said, exiting the car.

Waiting for him to open my door, I unbuckled my seatbelt reaching in the backseat to retrieve my overnight bag. He opened the door and I attempted to get out. He took the bag from my hand and helped me out. I waited for him to walk around me and followed him into the house.

"Hold on a minute. I have to make sure Lady don't come out jumping all on you."

"Lady? Who the hell is that?" I asked with a raised eyebrow.

"Lady is my Siberian Husky. She's still a baby at only seven months old. She's the only Lady in my life besides my mama," he said with a smirk, "and you, of course." He turned and hugged me, kissing my forehead.

He walked into the house and I heard the dog barking excitedly. I peeked in and she spotted me right off the bat. This dog looked like it was over forty pounds!

"G, I'm not coming in there. That's a big ass dog!" I shrieked.

He was laughing so hard that he was holding his stomach. "She's just a baby, Nova. She's not gonna do anything to you."

He came to the door and reached out for me. I took his hand but I didn't move.

"Sit, Lady, and stay," he said sternly. Lady sat as she was told and didn't move. I stepped up into the doorway and pulled G in front of me.

"Don't be scared, baby," he said, turning towards me.

"You have to trust me. You will be around Lady, so I want you to get used to her. Take my word that she is harmless," he said kissing my cheek.

I was scared, but I wanted to see what he was going to do. Once he saw that I was kind of settled, he spoke to Lady.

"Come here, Lady." The dog came to his side and stayed there.

"Hold out your hand so she can smell your scent. All she's gonna do is sniff you and she may lick your hand." he said never taking his eye off the dog.

I did as he asked and Lady did exactly what he said she would. When she was done, she wagged her tail and jumped all over me.

"Down, Lady, and goodnight."

She got down and turned and went down a flight of stairs, I assumed it was the basement.

"I'll give you a grand tour tomorrow, but right now let me get you to bed." Grabbing my bag, he led me to the stairs.

I thought he was going to escort me to the guest room, but the room we went to was very masculine. The room had a color theme of black and silver. He had a California king-sized bed to fit his 6'4" frame very comfortably, black silk sheets were on the bed with a lot of pillows. There was a sixty-five inch tv mounted on the wall and black carpet on the floor that your feet sunk into.

"G, how am I supposed to get into this damn bed? It is too high for me." I was sizing up this bed trying to figure out a way to get into it.

"I'll make sure you get in. Don't worry," he laughed. He went to his closet and came out with a black step stool in hand.

"I've never had to use this, but here you go, lil' bit."

"You mean to tell me that no other woman has had the privilege of using this stool to climb in your bed?" I asked.

"I can honestly say that you are the first woman besides family to ever step foot in this house, let alone this bed. I don't let just anyone come to my home. After my last relationship, which was many years ago, I bought this house. It's just been me and Lady" He walked over to me and picked me up, placing me on the bed.

"I'm gonna take a shower. I'll be back shortly. You can wait until I get out, join me, or use the bathroom down the hall. Your choice," he said with a smirk on his face.

As bad as I wanted to join him in the shower, I opted to use the bathroom down the hall.

"I'll use the other shower," I said, feeling my cheeks get rather hot.

***

I stepped out of the shower and proceeded to dry my body in the plush towel that I found in the linen closet. Removing my Shea butter lotion from my bag, I moisturized my skin. I looked in the mirror and stared at myself for a spell.

"I think I'm gonna keep my head shave on this side for a minute, it's kind of sexy," I said to myself. The gash has healed but I still apply the aloe to the scar so it won't be too noticeable. I brushed my teeth and flossed, and put on my soft bath robe.

127

I walked back down the hall to G's bedroom and damn near lost my breath. This man was standing with his back turned, towel wrapped around his waist and specks of water dripping down his back. The muscles that were protruding on every part of his body had my pussy leaking. I couldn't pry my eyes away if my life depended on it. That's how I got caught eye fuckin' his sexy ass.

"Do you like what you see, beautiful?" he asked without turning around.

How the hell did he know I was standing here fucking him every which way but up, in my mind? Shaking my head, I looked up at him and realized that he was looking at me the entire time through a mirror. I was so mesmerized that I didn't pay attention to that little, bitty detail.

It's time that I knock that cocky ass smirk off his face. I may be timid in the real world, but I don't play in the bedroom. Shit, I don't know who the hell I became at that moment. I placed my overnight bag on the chair by the door, walking seductively as I pulled the belt on my robe opening it up.

"The question is do you like what you see, Mr. Davenport?" I asked with my hand on my hip.

Letting the robe fall to the floor, G turned around slowly with the look of lust in his eyes. He walked over to me and lifted me above his head. My hands automatically went to the back of his head.

"Are you really ready to play this game, Miss Nova? There won't be any backing out. I love playing tit for tat baby," he said as he rubbed his nose back and forth between my lower lips.

I couldn't respond because I was still trying to fathom what was happening. I didn't expect him to react, but I guess when I showed my ass, literally, that meant game on. But I started it, now we were going to finish it.

"I'm ready, G," I whispered.

The words were barely audible, but he heard them. He dove in head first, dragging his tongue slowly down my slit. His lips wrapped around my pearl and he sucked lightly, that small action had me cummin' hard.

"Aaaaah, shit! Yes!" I screamed, grinding my pussy on his face.

"Mmmhmmm," he hummed, never coming up for air as he walked over to the bed and placed me down gently. He pulled up the stool and took a seat.

"I know you didn't think I was finished with your sexy ass, I'm just getting started," he said, nibbling on my inner thigh. My eyes closed and I arched my back, trying to meet his lips with my lower ones.

"Open your eyes, Nova. I want you to see me devour *my shit*."

Doing as I was told, he spread my legs as far as they would go. He inserted one finger into my love box followed by a second. I was so wet I heard my kitty swishing with every stroke. With his fingers still inserted in my pussy, he went right back to my center pulling my lips open with his other hand. He attacked her with a vengeance, covering my entire cookie with his mouth. His tongue was moving at a fast pace and I was on the brink of coming again.

"Right there, G! Yes, right there!"

He snatched his fingers out of my hole, tugging on my clit piercing while fucking me with his tongue. I couldn't hold back anymore at that point. My eyes rolled to the back of head and I squirted long and hard in his mouth.

"That's what the fuck I'm talking about," he said, kissing the top of my mound. "Now turn that ass around, baby. I need to see what them walls feel like."

I was exhausted from the head game he just put on me and my legs felt like jelly. I assumed the position, feeling him run his dick up and down my slit. Lubing up his dick with my juices, he went in quick and fast.

"Sssssss, shit! This pussy good, ma!" he said while he delivered slow strokes, gripping my waist.

He placed his leg on the bed and went in deep, hitting every organ in my mid section. All I could do was throw that ass back at him, meeting him stroke for stroke.

"Shit, G, yess! Fuck me, daddy! Fuck me!" And fucked me he did. He rolled me on my side, holding my left leg in the air, beating the fuck out of my pussy. He leaned in and started sucking my nipple, fucking me hard.

"This my pussy now, baby. I'm gonna take care of you and this pussy," he growled in my ear.

"Yes, it's yours, G! It's yours!" I screamed and at the same moment, we came together.

I hadn't had an orgasm like that in a long time. All I wanted to do now was sleep.

Chapter 25
G

I was knocked out with Nova laying on my chest when my phone started ringing. I looked down at her and she had her leg resting on top of my thigh. I didn't even care that she was slobbing on me. I put in that work, putting her ass to sleep. Shit, I couldn't begin to front, she wore my ass out, as well.

Reaching over to grab my phone, I saw that it was Avah calling. I silenced the phone and put it back down. It started ringing again and I had to count to ten to stop myself from getting mad. I hadn't heard from her in over a month and now she wanted to call a nigga at three in the fuckin' morning. Nah, I wasn't about to entertain that shit. I told her what I had to say when I spoke to her the last time. I couldn't understand why she wasn't getting it.

"G, answer your phone. It could be an emergency," Nova said without opening her eyes.

"Nah, that's Avah. Nothing good could come from that conversation if I answer, baby girl. So, I'll just let it ring." Avah called back a total of fifteen times in twenty minutes. She finally got the hint and stopped calling.

Nova turned over with her back facing me, with one leg bent and the other leg straight. I took that as an open invitation to get back in that pussy. Entering her wetness, I long stroked her until she started moaning. I placed my arm under her head and grabbed her by her neck. I squeezed just enough to get her turnt up. I fucked her so hard, I busted prematurely. I wanted it to last longer, but my dick had other plans. I cuddled next to her and fell asleep once again, never removing my dick from her tunnel.

My phone was ringing once again at six in the morning and I was beyond frustrated at this point. I rolled over and snatched it up. Looking at the screen, I saw that it was Scony.

"What up, Scony? What's going on?" I asked, rubbing sleep out of my eyes.

"I need you to get to the trap on the Nine. It's a bloodbath over here, brah. Somebody hit up the spot. Ricky got hit, Tyjuan is dead and Malikhi gone, too, brah."

I heard the hurt all in my nigga's voice. Malikhi was his little cousin that he helped raise. He wasn't even allowed to fuck with the shit that we do, so my mind was going, wondering what was he doing over there.

"Say less, my nigga. I'm on my way. You know what to do. Clear that muthafucka out before twelve get there."

I was scrambling around, trying to find something to put on. In the process, I saw Nova sitting up trying to figure out what was going on.

"We gon' find out who the fuck behind this shit. And when we do, you already know how it's about to go down." I disconnected the call and threw my phone on the bed.

I grabbed a black hoodie, a pair of black sweats and my black Air Force Ones, and went to the bathroom to take care of my hygiene quickly. As I was brushing my teeth, Nova appeared in the doorway.

"What's going on, G? Is everything alright?" she nervously asked.

"Nah, baby girl. Everything's not ok, but I'll explain everything when I come back. You're good staying here, right? I'll make sure Lady stays outside until I return," I said, rinsing my mouth as I looked through the mirror.

"Yeah, I'll be alright and you don't have to do that. Lady will be just fine. Make sure she has food and leave the rest to me. But I want you to be safe, ok?"

"No doubt, babe," I said, walking back into my room going to the closet.

Opening the hidden door that housed my safe and my gun collection, I grabbed my Sig Sauer P226 and tucked it in the gun holster that I had under my hoodie. Placing an extra magazine in my pocket, I was ready to roll. I snatched my phone off the bed and kissed Nova on the lips.

"I'll be back soon, baby. Keep it warm for me. You have everything you need here, but you can call Mo and Jae to keep you company. I'll call you to make sure you're ok."

Hugging her tightly, I didn't want to let her go but I had to get out of there.

"Get you some more sleep. I'm out," I said, pecking her lips once more.

Meesha

Chapter 26
Scony

I couldn't believe some muthafucka had enough balls to come through my shit and air it out. We didn't have beef with none of these niggas out here, yet and still my lil' cousin is lying outside this bitch with a sheet over his face. The tears wouldn't stop falling, but I had to dead this shit quick. I'm a muthafuckin' goon in these streets and these niggas about to feel it.

"You a'ight, my nigga?" Quan asked when he walked up.

"Nah, man. I'm not alright! My lil' nigga gone, man. He was only seventeen muthafuckin' years old. I was raising that nigga to be better than me. What the fuck was he doing over here is what I want to know! But on top of all that, I wanna know who the fuck did this shit!"

The police were deep around this muthafucka and we were ducked off in the crowd. Wasn't nobody saying shit to they ass, but somebody was gonna talk to my black ass once they leave. I looked down the street and saw G pull up. I shot that nigga a text to leave his heat in the car. The last thing I needed was his ass to get locked up.

The coroner was loading the bodies in the van as he was walking up.

"This shit is fucked up, my nigga. What's the word?" G asked, looking around.

"Ain't shit being said right now, fam. These muthafuckin' pigs mad as fuck because ain't nobody talking. They don't know shit about the robbery, so they're not saying anything about going inside. They were shot outside."

"Well, they need to wrap this shit up so I can get some fuckin' answers! What's the word on Ricky?" he asked, still scooping out the scene.

"Antonio is at the hospital with him. They ain't gave an update yet, but that nigga was conscious when they put him in the ambulance. He was hit in the side," I explained.

"What the fuck was Malikhi doing over here? Damn man, did you call Lovely yet?"

I was silent, fighting back tears. I couldn't do nothing but shake my head.

"You didn't call her, Scony? She should've been the first one you called, fam! Get ya muthafuckin' mind right. She should be down here, man." G was pissed, but he didn't understand.

"Nah, I didn't call her, G. This shit is about to fuck her up, man. I just got her off that shit, man. But I'm gonna swing by the house and tell her face to face. Then take her down to the morgue to identify him."

"A'ight, nigga. I'm gonna ride with ya. Quan, I'm gon' need you to stay here and try to get as much information as you can. I know this bitch wasn't deserted when the shit went down. Pull the muthafuckin' tapes! I know for a fact them shits gonna tell something. As a matter of fact, it will tell it all. Fuck questioning these niggas until after we see that shit."

"A'ight, bet. I'll be able to go in soon, twelve packin' up as we speak. Y'all gon' 'head and get Love. Meet me back at the warehouse in Markham," Quan said, looking around.

"A'ight, bet."

We dapped Quan up and went to G's car. I'll come back for my shit later.

***

G pulled up to Lovely's house and before we could get out, she was running out of the door.

"How you let them kill my baby, Scony? You said you were gonna keep him out the streets!" Lovely ran up to me, beating me in my chest. I couldn't do nothing but let her get that shit off. In her eyes, this was all my fault. Even though I know for a fact this was not on me, I let her place the blame.

I wrapped my arms around her and I let her cry, but at the same time I was restraining her from hitting me again.

"Love, man, I didn't even know Khi was over there. I always told him to stay the fuck away from seventy-ninth street. Ain't shit but trouble over there. Do you know why he was over there?" I asked that question, hoping she had an answer and she did.

"Malikhi has been hanging around the Nine for weeks now, Scony. Yo' ass ain't been around this muthafucka lately. He's been hangin' out with Ricky and nem. I tried putting his ass on punishment, but he sneaks out. I don't give his ass money, but he always seems to have lots of it. I found muthafuckin' heroine in his fuckin closet, Scony! When I brought it to him, that muthafucka slapped me, took his shit and left."

I was shocked as hell by the things she just laid on me. This lil' nigga was out here trying to be in these streets after I explained to him why he shouldn't. A hard head makes a soft ass. But one of them niggas from the Nine was going to answer to me, because I told they ass to send him the fuck on if he ever came that way.

"Why the fuck you didn't call me, Lovely?" I asked, lifting her head. Something wasn't right because she couldn't look me in my face.

"Why the fuck didn't you call me, Lovely!" I yelled, while shaking her ass.

"Hold up, fam. Calm yo' ass down and let her answer the fucking question. You can't let yo' emotions speak for you right now." G grabbed my arm, stopping me from shaking her ass.

"I didn't call you because—because, I didn't want you to find out I was using again."

She said that shit low as hell stuttering, but I heard every word and every syllable that dropped from her mouth.

"Say that shit again, Love."

I was trying to stop my blood from boiling, but there was no coming back from it this time. My blood pressure was through the roof.

"Tell me I didn't hear you say what the fuck I thought I heard, Lovely. Was Khi supplying you with dope in exchange for him to run wild?" I grabbed her chin and forced her to look at me. When I looked in her eyes, her pupils were dilated and red as fuck.

"Yo' ass high right now! All the money I put into getting your ass clean and you go right back to it! Why, Lovely? Why, man!"

At that point, I couldn't stop the tears from falling. I was hurt to my core with everything that has happened this morning.

"I'm sorry, Scony. I swear to you I am so sorry! I didn't mean for none of this to happen. I allowed him to go out and do what he wanted to do. Yes, he supplied me with the dope that I needed. I was sick without it, Scony. That rehab center was a temporary fix. I only did it because you asked me to."

She was crying uncontrollably and I didn't even want to look at her anymore. I turned to walk away, but stopped in my tracks.

"We are about to go to this morgue to identify my lil' cousin's remains. Then we are gonna get through the arrangements and the funeral. After that, you can do what the fuck you wanna do. I'm not about to try to help a muthafucka that don't wanna help their self. That's not how I operate. Now get the fuck in the car so we can go."

Chapter 27
G

Leaving the morgue, my mind was all fucked up. It hurt to see my lil' nigga lying on that cold ass table, riddled with bullets. Malikhi was shot eight times in his torso. He didn't stand a chance. Seeing my bro Scony breakdown like a baby brought tears to my eyes. Malikhi meant the world to that nigga and nothing good was gonna come out of this situation. The niggas that did this shit better be on the first thing smokin' out of this bitch.

"Scony, we gotta go back in and get Malikhi. Do you think they are gonna let him go home when he wakes up?" Lovely kept looking back at the building, stopping every five steps to go back.

"He ain't coming back, Lovely. Malikhi is gone, cuz. He's dead." Scony tried to hug her, but she pushed him away.

"He ain't dead! Why the fuck y'all keep saying that? Go back and get my baby, Scony!!" Lovely broke down right there in the parking lot. I had to pick her up and carry her the rest of the way.

I sat in the backseat with her while Scony drove back to Lovely's house. When we pulled up, she was sleeping. I got out the car first, went around and lifted her out, carrying her into the house. Walking in, her boyfriend Jerome was in the midst of hitting the glass dick.

Scony was on his ass, beating the fuck out him. Jerome fell on the floor and Scony started stomping his head into the floor. The shit happened so fast, I didn't have time to react. By the time I laid Lovely on the couch, that nigga wasn't moving. I grabbed Scony and pushed him out the door.

"Nigga, I know you are pissed, but this ain't the way to do this shit!" I screamed at him.

"G, I ain't trying to hear none of that, my nigga. *That nigga* is the reason she can't leave that shit alone. *That nigga* is the reason my lil' cousin is laid up in a muthafuckin freezer in the county morgue! Get the fuck outta here with that soft shit! This ain't the time to be rational, my nigga, it's war time. Either you with me or against me!" he spat.

I understood where he was coming from with what he said, and I couldn't do nothing but respect him for what he did. He did it out of love for his family.

"You already know that I'm with you, my nigga, but what good you gon' be locked the fuck up because you're wearing your feelings on your sleeve? You ain't the only one hurt behind Malikhi, nigga. He was my family, too. I'm not mad because you fucked that nigga up at all. It's a time and a place for that shit."

I reached in my pocket and threw him my keys. "Go to the car and blow something. I'm about to go clean shit up and call the ambulance for this nigga."

When I walked back in the house, Jerome was at the kitchen sink rinsing his face. I walked over to him.

"I'm gonna say this one time and one time only nigga, if I hear about you giving Lovely any type of drug, I'm gon' murk yo' ass. You two stupid muthafuckas worried about getting high and not paying attention to the shit that mattered—"

"G, I didn't have shit to do with that!"

This nigga had the audacity to cut me the fuck off. I snatched my tool off my hip and stuffed it in this nigga mouth.

"If you ever in life interrupt me when I'm talking again, I'll end yo' fuckin' life, bitch. Now when I'm talkin', you muthafuckin' listen. Like I said, if I find out you are feeding her that bullshit, I'm gonna splatter yo' muthafuckin' brains all over Chicago. If she talk about it, you better act like a fuckin counselor and steer her in the right direction. Do you fuckin' hear me, muthafucka?"

This nigga was so scared he was pissing on himself, but I know his ass got the memo because his head was bobbing up and down.

"I'm taking all drugs and paraphernalia out of this bitch. You will never know when I'll show up. Now, not only do you have to worry about Scony, but you got to worry about me too! Call the muthafuckin' ambulance and take your stupid ass to the hospital. And I don't have to coach you on what to say to them muthafuckas, right? Let the law show up looking for me. They'll be back to pick yo' azz up, putting you in a body bag."

I removed my gun from his mouth and wiped it off on his shirt. Walking around scooping shit off the table, I went into both bedrooms and found shit there, too. I searched everywhere until I collected everything.

"Don't forget what the fuck I said, pussy." I said, pointing at Jerome, before I turned and walked out of that muthafucka.

***

I didn't realize how late it had gotten. It was after one in the afternoon and I hadn't checked on my future. I took out my phone and dialed her number. She picked up on the second ring.

"Hey, G, are you alright?" she asked.

"Yeah, I'm ok, baby. Shit is hectic right now, but I'll try to be back as soon as I can. I just wanted to call and check on you. How are you feeling, beautiful?"

"I'm doing alright now that I've talked to you. I'm just laying here with my new best friend, Lady," she said chuckling.

"Nova baby, Lady better not be in my damn bed. She knows that's not happening."

"Uh oh. Lady, you gotta get down, boo. Daddy said you can't be in the bed."

I heard Lady whining in the background and started laughing.

"Don't be spoiling my dog, Nova. I'm not havin' that shit either. What do you want to eat? I'll stop and get something on the way home. The thing is, I don't know when I'll be there."

Smacking her lips, she said, "Boy, please. I have everything laid out for dinner already. I decided to make lasagna, sweet peas, a salad and garlic bread. You don't have to stop to get anything."

"Oh shit. Let me find out you know how to throw down in the kitchen. Gon' make a nigga marry your ass," I said, laughing.

"Boy, bye. Be safe out there, G, and hurry back." She was pouting and I could tell, it was all in her voice.

"I'm gon' show yo' ass when I get there that I ain't no damn boy. Shid, I proved that shit last night. I guess I'm gon' have to show you again. But on that note, keep it warm for me, baby. I'll see you soon."

I let her hang up first and placed my phone back on my hip, but before I could take my hand away it was ringing again. I retrieved it and saw Antonio calling.

"What's up, cuz? Give me some good news."

"Aye, I need you to come to Christ Hospital. Ricky is awake. I'll fill y'all in when you get here. How's Scony?" he asked with much concern.

"He's hanging in there. This shit got his head all fucked up, but we are about to come through there," I said, walking towards the car.

"A'ight, bet."

When I got to the car, Scony was still smoking. I know he done blazed up back to back, but I'm gonna let him do what he needs to do to clear his mind. I got in my whip and started that bitch up.

"What's the word, big homie?" he asked in between pulls.

"Tonio just called and said Ricky is woke. We about to ride through and find out what the fuck happened," I said, pulling off.

Scony was zoned out until his phone rang. He didn't even attempt to answer it. That's how I knew my nigga was in a dark place. His phone rang again and he pulled it out, looking at the screen and answered it.

"What's good, shorty? I'm good, dealing with some shit right nah. I'on know, I'll hit you later and let you know. A'ight, bet." He put the phone between his legs and continued to smoke. I didn't know who had called, but they didn't cheer him up at all.

We pulled up to the hospital and found a parking spot. I hit Tonio up and asked what room he was in. He gave me the information that I needed and we got out. When we got in the hospital we got our passes and went up to the room. Ricky was propped up, eating jello and talking to Tonio.

"What up, y'all. Man, Scony I'm sorry about Malikhi, man. I swear I told fam on too many occasions to stay the fuck away from the Nine, but he wouldn't listen." Ricky was talking faster than the roadrunner and that nigga didn't even talk.

"If he was coming through there Ricky. Why I didn't know about it? I told all you niggas before hand to inform me if he came around."

Scony was calm talking to Ricky. I was surprised.

"I fucked up when I didn't tell you, but I thought he wasn't coming through no mo' because I didn't see him again until today. When he came through, he knocked on the door and we all came out. I asked him what the fuck was he doing over there, but he didn't get the chance to answer because out of nowhere this black Chevy came gunnin' down the street. Them niggas just started shooting. It was like they knew what they were doing. Malikhi took majority of the bullets because he was standing in front of us. I got hit in the side and fell. TyJuan went down with a bullet to his head. Them niggas jumped out and stood over us. I played dead like a mutha-fucka, but I couldn't move for real. Then they went into the trap and came back out with about four duffle bags. That was a lick, my nigga," he said, spooning jello into his mouth.

"You said it was a black Chevy?" I asked, scratching my head. Both Scony and Antonio was looking at me, probably putting this shit together just like I was.

"Yeah, it was an old ass hooptie, but I know it was a Chevy for sure."

"Hold up. Didn't them niggas that shot up Nova's crib get in an old Chevy?" Antonio asked.

"Hell yeah! This nigga been missing in action, laying low then had the nerve to come for my people. I'm about to paint this muthafucka red. Stay up, lil' homie. Hit my line if you need anything. We got to go find this muthafucka." I said to Ricky.

Scony was ready to paint the city red, too, and he wasn't gonna stop until we killed everybody involved.

Chapter 28
Kelvin

Them muthafuckas thought a nigga was pussy. They had muthafuckas watching my mom's and my sister crib, so I stopped going to their houses. I didn't want that kind of heat coming their way. I've just been laying low on the west side with Sergio and them niggas. When I'm at the crib, I'd been kickin' it with Ziva. Her muthafuckin ass been in her feelings over some shit that Monica's fat ass said to her, so she hadn't even spoke to Nova.

But she still came through on some shit. She befriended this bitch named Avah that was fucking with G. He stopped answering the bitch calls, so she big mad. Her and Ziva got tight on the count of me because the bitch was drooling over a nigga when I rolled down on Z at a restaurant. I bought their food and rolled out.

Later that night, Z hit me up talking about ole girl wanted to get down. I was for it, so I met them at ole girl crib. I remember that night like it was yesterday.

When I pulled up to the address that Z sent to my phone, I texted her and told her I was outside. She came down and opened the door, babygirl lived on the third floor. Once we got inside, she wasn't even trying to talk. I didn't know what the fuck Z told her about me, but shorty went straight for the zipper. I guess there was no introductions needed. She freed my dick and slurped his ass right up. Bitch was sucking my dick so good, she had me on my tippy toes.

"Damn, shorty! Suck that shit!" I said through clenched teeth while holding the back of her head.

She didn't have anything on, but a thong and heels. Ziva looked like she was getting mad, so I motioned her over and kissed her.

"You miss daddy, huh? I said, pulling her tank top over her head. This bitch, Avah, didn't let go of the dick though.

Ziva stepped out of her boy shorts and placed my hand on her clit. I rubbed her until she was soaked.

"Get behind her and suck that pussy, Z."

Me and Ziva did this type of shit all the time. We pulled bitches together on a regular. I was leaning against the wall while this bitch had my python in a death grip.

Ziva got behind all that ass and buried her face deep in that shit. Avah was moaning loud as fuck, so I knew baby girl was eating the shit out of them cookies. I almost popped my top when she came up and started eating the booty like groceries. She turned over on her back and pulled Avah's kitty down to her mouth. I had to get in on that. I tapped shorty on her head so she would release that grip. I walked over to Ziva and positioned myself between her legs and tore that pussy up.

We kept switching positions until the next morning and that's when baby girl started telling all the business on where that nigga G's spots were. What would you do for the dick?

Avah was a cool chic, but I needed her for one thing and one thing only. Once I had the information I needed to put my plan in motion, it was on. I ran the shit down to Sergio and we scoped the trap out for weeks. The niggas they had working out of that trap didn't pay attention to shit. I knew that this was gonna be like taking candy from a baby.

They were always turning up in the wee hours of the morning, attention span on zero. I knew that was the time we had to hit 'em. We went through there and aired that bitch out, running up in that muthafucka. The door to the room that everything was in was locked, but once I shot that bitch open it was a big payday for us. We cleaned that muthafucka out completely. And on top of that, we killed them muthafuckas.

We went back to the westside and divided all that shit up equally, it was time to get paid. Word on the street was one of the niggas that we hit was Scony's cousin. That's another notch on my belt because I hit them niggas where it hurted. I didn't feel guilty about killing an innocent muthafucka, because I owed that shit to his cousin for being in my business.

"Nigga, do you know that these niggas on the prowl right now? They don't even know where to fuckin' look, but I'm about to get rich off they shit. On top of that, we clipped two hunnid grand off these niggas."

Sergio was running his fuckin' mouth in front of niggas that didn't need to know what the fuck went down.

"Man, shut yo' muthafuckin' mouth! You ain't new to this shit! You are talking too muthafuckin' much," I said, snapping on his ass.

"You right, but these niggas ain't gon' say shit."

All I could do was shake my fuckin' head. My phone rang and it was Ziva.

"What up, Z?" I said, watching the shit going on around me.

"I'm about to pull up. You got that for me?"

"Yeah, I got it. Come through," I said hanging up.

When she pulled up, I went to the car and got in.

"We did that shit, baby girl. This was the first hit, but not the last. So be on your toes and be ready to go when I call. Don't try to bail out on me, Z."

I looked her in the eyes to see if I saw even a hint of deception because I won't have a problem peeling her muthafuckin' wig back.

"I'm gonna be ready, but I got some news for you. Scony searching hard for whoever hit them. Please be careful, Kels. When they come, they are coming hard so watch yourself," she said, looking sad.

"You watch yourself, too, Z. Call me when you get to your destination, shorty."

I got out the car, grabbed my shit out of the crib and went to talk to Sergio.

"Yo, bro, I'm about to blow this joint. Be on the watch. Them niggas looking for us. Be easy, Sergio. This is just the beginning, baby. We got more to do."

"Hell yeah! We do, nigga! I'll get up with ya man."

We dapped up and I hopped in my ride and peeled off. I was feeling really good about this shit. Niggas ain't gone know what hit 'em next time around.

Chapter 29
Quan

I was sitting at this monitor going through the footage non-stop, I couldn't see shit. These niggas came through and cleaned house. I knew I was missing something, but I didn't know what that something was. I had to go through that shit one more time. I started the video back to the point where the niggas rolled up. They jumped out the car blasting with the intention to kill everything moving. They hit Malikhi head on, this was gonna be hard for Scony to watch.

Next, there was a shot that hit TyJuan, a straight head shot. He dropped right where he stood. Ricky was the last to get shot and he laid there playing dead like he said. Nobody had time to pull their tools out at all because they weren't on their shit. The footage when the niggas went in the trap was where I needed to pay close attention. They didn't have on any gloves, but they had on masks. I slowed that shit down and watched carefully, trying to see what these niggas touched.

As I watched, one of these niggas took his mask off! I was excited as hell to see that. I zoomed in on the nigga, but I didn't recognize his ass. He was a big, burly Puerto Rican nigga. He had tats on his hands that I could see vividly. I screenshoted all that shit and saved it. Grabbing for my phone, I hit G's line. He answered with no hesitation.

"Yo, G. Where ya at, my nigga? I found something, man. Get to the warehouse now!" I spat.

"We in route to you as we speak. As a matter of fact, we'll be there in five," G said, hanging up.

Less than five minutes later, these niggas were practically running into the Dungeon as we called it. I met them as they were coming in.

"Did you ever get a hit on that partial license plate from the shooting at Nova's crib, Q?"

"I didn't get anything yet, fam. That car is not coming up nowhere. But I was looking at the footage and I saw some shit that may help us, come on in the office and look," I said with excitement.

We walked to the back of the Dungeon, I sat down and ran the footage from the point when they were in the trap. I slowed it down when the Puerto Rican nigga took off his mask and paused it.

"Do y'all know this nigga?" I asked, looking around.

G's nostrils flared and he said, "Yeah, that's this lame muthafucka named Sergio. His ass been lowkey hatin' on a nigga since I told him he didn't have what it took to be on my team. We got one identified and his ass gonna tell me who else was involved before I send his stupid ass to meet his maker," G said, staring a hole into the computer screen.

"I got word from one of them lil' niggas that was outside on the Nine this morning, saying that a cat named Conte wanted to holla at y'all about the shooting at the club. I told him I would let y'all know and set something up. You want me to have him come through now?"

"Are you out of your fuckin' mind, Q? What kind of information this muthafucka got that couldn't be told a month ago? I don't trust no fuckin' body and neither should you! Don't ever invite a muthafucka where you shit at. Especially if you don't know shit about the nigga."

"Tell that nigga to meet us at GSpot in an hour. Right now, I need to look at the whole footage from today," Scony said, sitting down.

"Fam, I don't think that's a good idea. I mean it's too soon to—" I said, trying to talk him out of watching.

"That's why I really don't give a fuck what you think! Run that shit. Case closed," he said, cutting me off as he folded his arms across his chest. G nodded his head and I ran the tape back.

I watched the tape already, so I was just watching Scony's reaction. I saw his face change from anger when the car pulled up, to horror when the niggas jumped out making their guns sing, to finally sorrow when Malikhi's body was riddled with the bullets. Scony jumped up and punched the concrete walls over and over, busting his knuckles open.

"They shot him down like a fuckin' animal! He didn't deserve that shit, man! When I find these muthafuckas they are dying slow my nigga!" Tears were streaming down his face and he dropped to his knees. All we could do was give him that time to let it out.

I took that opportunity to call the nigga named Conte. I got up and stepped out into the main part of the warehouse away from Scony's breakdown. The phone rang and he answered right before the voicemail picked up.

"Yeah," he said into the phone.

"Aye, this is Quan. G is gonna meet you at GSpot in an hour. Don't come on no bullshit, my nigga. Straight up."

"Nah, man, it ain't even like that. I just want to get this information off my chest. I know that I'm right about what I saw, so there won't be no type of bullshit involved. But I'll be there and thanks, man," he said, hanging up.

Dude sound like he's on the up and up, but like G said, too much shit had happened and this wasn't the time to be trusting random muthafuckas. But we would see what the fuck it was once we meet up with this nigga. I walked back into the office and G was talking to Scony.

"I promise you, my nigga, we gon' settle this shit once and for all. You ain't by yourself with this shit. When one hurt, we all hurt. Malikhi was family to all of us, bro. Believe that."

G grabbed Scony in a man hug.

"Now shake that shit off, go clean ya hands up and let's go see what this muthafucka got for us."

***

When we pulled up to GSpot, a tall nigga got out of his ride. Everybody upped their tools, ready to make this nigga fish food.

"Hold up, my niggas. I'm Conte! Don't shoot!" he pleaded with his hands in the air.

Just because this nigga stated who he was, didn't mean shit to us. Our guns stayed on point. G was the only one that lowered his shit. but kept his bitch by his side.

Walking over to the nigga he said, "Turn the fuck around! And don't make no sudden moves or you will have a bullet in your head faster than Usain Bolt, my nigga."

He started patting his ass down. Conte didn't have anything on him, so G put his Nina away.

"Man, I told y'all I wasn't on no bullshit. I almost pissed on myself." This scary ass nigga had the nerve to let us know how spooked he was, pussy ass.

"Aye, ain't no muthafuckin' trust out here in these streets. One day you will learn that shit. Every nigga ain't man friendly, nigga. Take yo' ass on to the club," Scony spat at this dude, giving him a little bit of knowledge.

We walked into the club behind G. It was now six o'clock in the evening on a Tuesday, happy hour was in full effect. We passed the patrons in the club and went straight upstairs to talk business.

"What you got for us playa?" G asked, sitting on the edge of his desk. He looked at this nigga like he was waiting on him to say some bullshit that wasn't gonna help us.

"The night of the shooting, I was chillin' with this female named Ziva in the back corner of the club. She was texting on her phone while talking to me and I spoke on it. She said someone was calling, but I knew that was a lie. She turned her back and raised her phone. I know she took a pic of something, but I don't know of what. Then she sent a text to somebody and started smirking while looking at the dance floor." He paused for a second then continued.

"About fifteen minutes later, we were in a deep conversation when she just paused. Something caught her attention, then she got this horrid expression on her face. I asked her what was up but she didn't hear me. She then tried to get through the crowd and that's when the shots rang out. It's like she knew what was about to happen." He stopped talking and was just shaking his head.

"So, you said this bitch name is Ziva? Or is that the name she gave to your ass?" Scony asked Conte.

"Yeah, that's her name, man. I grew up with Z and Sabrina— I mean Nova," he said, correcting himself. "I learned that she changed her name that night. Z was side-eyeing her all night, dragging her name through the mud the whole time we were talking."

G stood up and paced back and forth, rubbing his hand over his face. "Tell me this. If you felt that Ziva had something to do with what happened, why didn't you say something back then? Why come out with it now?"

"When I found out that Nova was shot, I ran into her ex, Kels, one day over on the west side. I asked him how was she and he didn't know. But he didn't seem to feel bad about her getting shot though. Then he said something like, 'that's what that bitch get for crossing the wrong muthafucka'. I couldn't believe he said something like that. Then he got a call and I heard him say Ziva's name. That's when I put two and two together they were in on that shit together." This dude seemed solid with what he was saying. I believed his ass.

"You telling me that this bitch set her own best friend up? I can't see her doing this out of jealousy. That was shit brutal! Nova could have been killed!" G screamed.

"G, it makes sense actually, bro," Scony said, looking him in his face.

"When we met Nova, Mo, and Jade, Ziva wasn't around at the club that night. She wasn't at the hospital with the rest of us when Nova was brought in either. And she damn sure ain't never been by anyone's house because the ladies would have mentioned it. As a matter of fact, we ain't heard shit from her since Nova's house got shot up." Scony said that last part slow as hell looking directly at G.

"G, that shit wasn't a coincidence. That bitch called them niggas after Mo read her ass!" Scony was mad as hell because he was getting closer and closer to the muthafuckas that shot his cousin.

"Ain't this a bitch! That snake muthafucka! How the fuck could she bite the fuckin' hand that fed her for years?" Antonio spats. We all was mad about this situation. Bitches kill me with the bullshit they be on.

"Ummm, I think there is something else y'all should know," Conte said, breaking up the small chatter that was going on around the room. All eyes were on him at his point.

"I was chillin' on Division with some cats that I'm cool with and they were talking about a lick they pulled off. They were moreso bragging, talking about how they got this female name Avah to tell them what they needed to know—" Conte was interrupted by G's sudden outburst.

"That bitch Avah got a hand in this shit, too! Yeah, a bitch gets real grimey when you snatch the dick away. I'm gonna pay her ass a personal visit. Keep going, my nigga." G was huffin' and puffin' like a pit bull ready to attack.

"Yeah, they were saying that Kels and Ziva got the information out of her somehow. This nigga named Sergio was running his mouth about all the drugs and money he got off the shit. But the shit that took me by surprise was him admitting he shot the kid over there on Seventy-ninth. I know the kid was one of y'all family and I had to let this shit out. I couldn't keep this shit to myself. They know where all y'all spots are and they are planning another hit," Conte said looking around the room.

"Them muthafuckas are gonna come through and get their shit blown back. It won't be successful the second time around," G said, walking over to the surveillance equipment.

"I'm about to run this tape back to that night. Point this bitch out for me. And I'm gonna need the names of the other muthafuckas that was with them," G said, pressing play. Conte got up to move closer to the screen and watched carefully. He pointed out Ziva as the ladies entered the club. Then we watched her reaction before, during, and after the shooting. We had all we needed right here after looking through it again.

"Aye, give the location on that bitch nigga Sergio and anything you got on Kels and Ziva," Antonio said to Conte. He gave up the information he had with no problem,

"Thanks, man, for bringing that information to us. Now if I find out your ass was a part of this bullshit, I bet not ever run into your ass again. If I do it's gonna be lights out, my nigga," Scony said with his gun in Conte's face.

Meesha

Chapter 30
Antonio

It had been a long ass week for our crew. We all took our share of responsibilities to plan this funeral for Malikhi. We weren't gonna let our nigga deal with this by himself. It's bad enough Lovely's ass has been missing in action and the funeral is in the morning. Scony and Quan had been beating the city looking for her and that nigga was pissed.

I just finished dropping Malikhi's clothes off at the funeral home, now I'm on my way to spend some much-needed time with Monica. We hadn't said anything to any of the ladies about what we found out. It was going to crush them. The information that nigga Conte gave us panned out. Sergio's bitch ass had been flossing all week, being extra flashy. He better enjoy that shit because his days are numbered.

Kels, Kelvin, or whatever the fuck he goes by, been ducked off somewhere. Ain't nobody heard or seen this nigga period. That bitch, Ziva, hadn't been spotted either. The only one that's still making noise is that crazy bitch, Avah. She had been blowing up G's phone doing the most, not knowing her ass was being sized up for a pine box soon.

In twenty-four hours, shit was about to get real for a lot of mufuckas. We just wanted to lay the lil' homie down and send him off in style, before we made the CPD earn their take. Shit wasn't going to be nothing nice in the Chi once we change from suits to all black war gear. My phone rang, bringing me out of my thoughts. I looked down at the display and it was Mo calling.

"What's up, sexy," I said with a big ass, kool-aid grin on my face.

"Are you still coming over? I just wanted to make sure you didn't forget about me," she said flirtatiously.

"I can never forget about your little cute ass, baby. I'm about to pull off now. I had to drop some shit off at the funeral home for Scony," I explained.

"Oh, ok. Well, I'm waiting on you, handsome. I made us a light lunch, so I hope you're hungry."

"I'm hungry, but not for food. Is there anything else on the menu?" I asked, laughing.

She was silent for a moment, but her comeback game was smooth.

"It can be. How about an open salad bar?" she chuckled.

"You want a nigga to eat the booty, huh? Yeah, I knew yo ass was a freak, but I'll see what I can do about that. I want you to be butt naked when I get there. I'll call you when I'm about to pull up, so you can have the door open. Then I want you to be on all fours with that ass in the air, so I won't have to wait." My dick was hard just thinking about the shit I was about to do to baby girl. I've been waiting patiently for this shit.

I stopped at a red light, grooving to some old school Tupac when I looked to my left. I had to do a double take because the bitch that we had been looking for was right there in plain sight. I was mad as hell because I had pussy waiting on me, but I couldn't pass up the opportunity to follow this bitch.

The light turned green and she pulled off. I signaled to get in the lane she was in. I was following her at a safe distance. The bitch didn't know shit about watching her surroundings. I'm gonna make sure Monica knows all about that shit. The way my life is set up, she will be well prepared.

We had been driving for a little minute, when she turned into an apartment complex on 144th & Parnell in Riverdale. She got out of her car and went into the apartment building, 14423. I took down her plate number and the make and model of her car and drove off.

I called Mo. I had to explain why I was late. When she answered, she didn't sound upset. I liked that shit.

"Hey, baby. I had a little detour to make, but I'm in route right now."

"Okay, I'm here waiting on you. I'll see you when you get here," she said, shuffling around.

"Ok, baby. I'll be there shortly," I said. ending the call.

I had about a twenty-minute ride to get to her crib. I'm gonna try to cut it to ten or fifteen. While I drove, I called G to tell him what I found out.

"Yo, what up, cuz. What you on?" he asked.

"Shit, I'm on my way to Monica's crib, but I had to call you and tell you who I saw today."

"Talk to me nigga, I'm waiting. Hold on a minute."

He put the phone down and I heard someone giggling in the background, then a loud moan. Shaking my head, I hung up on that nasty muthafucka. How the fuck he gon' put me on hold to play in pussy?

A few minutes later he called back and I answered. "What, nigga!" I said, acting like I was mad.

"My bad, cuz. You weren't supposed to witness that shit," he said, laughing. Who the fuck did you see today?"

"I saw that bitch, Ziva, dog. I followed her to this apartment complex in Riverdale. I don't know if it's her place, but I do know it's one of the spots she be."

"That's good shit, my nigga! We goin' in on these pussy muthafuckas tomorrow night. Ain't no mo' delays after we lay lil' homie down. These streets gon' know not to fuck with us after this shit. We ain't had to lay a nigga down in a minute, my trigga finger itching. But let me get back to my future and I'll hit you up later," he said.

"A'ight, fo sho, my nigga. Be safe."

I was about five minutes from Monica's house and I shot her a text.

Me: *I'm about to pull up. I'm coming in to mark my territory, so be ready.*

Mo: *Door open. Get in where you fit in, playa. Lol.*

That's the shit I'm talking about! I'm about to tear that ass up.

Chapter 31
Scony

I spent all day and night looking for Lovely and she hasn't been seen, anywhere. It was six in the morning and Malikhi's funeral was set to begin at eleven. On one hand I was pissed, but on the other I was worried about her ass. I hoped when she showed up, she would be sober. I knew this shit was eating her alive, because it was surely trying to eat at my soul. I went to her house and sat in Malikhi's room and cried until my eyes wouldn't form another tear.

I sat and thought about how I was gonna torture the shit out of the niggas that took my cousin from me. I sat there hitting a blunt and sipping on Henny, I heard the front door open and closed. I knew for a fact that it was Lovely, but I didn't move. I watched the door, pulling my glock and put it in my lap just in case.

Lovely walked in the room and stopped and gasped, holding her chest. She flipped the light switched on and let out a sigh of relief.

"Scony, you scared the shit out of me. Why are you sitting in here with the lights off?"

"I'm just sitting here chillin' and thinking, Love. I've been looking all over for you since last week. Where have you been?" I asked, taking a sip from my cup.

"I knew I couldn't go see my baby for the last time high Scony, so I went to a program on my own. They allowed me to come out for the day to attend the services. I didn't want you to know because I had to do this on my own," she said silently crying.

"I'm proud of you, man. That was a big step you took. I want you to stick with it this time, Love. You went out and did this shit on your own, so you must want to change your life around," I said, standing up.

"I didn't do it on my own, Scony. My baby was the voice of reason. When we left the morgue and y'all brought me home, I was sleeping when it happened. Malikhi came to me in my dream, Scony. I felt him touching me. I smelled his Axe body wash. He told me that he wanted me to clean myself up and he would be right beside me every step of the way. He told me how sorry he was for leaving me and that he loved me. When I reached out to touch him, he disappeared. I got up and went to the very rehab center I had left and checked myself back in."

Lovely was crying, leaning against the doorframe for balance. I walked over to her and wrapped her in my arms.

"I know I said some harsh words to you that day, cuz. I was very disappointed in you. Everything I said, I meant every word. I won't take them back either. But today, I can honestly say that I'm very proud of you. Fight, Love. Fight for you and for Malikhi. You can do it," I said, shedding a couple tears of my own.

I let her go and looked down at her. "Fight, man. I need you to fight this shit," I said, kissing her forehead.

"I want you to go in there and get some sleep. We are leaving about ten thirty, so be ready," I said, walking back to the chair by the window.

"Scony, I don't have anything to wear today."

"Yes, you do. Everything you need is in your room. Don't try to cop out, Love. You're going to say your last goodbye and I'll be right there with you." I said, looking out the window.

***

The time was nine-thirty and I still hadn't made any attempts to get dressed. I was trying to be strong for Lovely, but I was weak as fuck. I wasn't ready to see my lil' homie like that. My body just wouldn't cooperate with me. My stomach was in knots and I was shaking uncontrollably. I laid down and closed my eyes trying to calm myself, but it wasn't working at all.

Knock, knock.

Someone was knocking on the door, but I didn't even acknowledge that shit. I didn't want to be bothered.

Bam, Bam, Bam!

"Scony, open this fuckin' door before I kick it off the hinges nigga!" G's ass was the culprit behind all that damn banging. I got up to unlock and open the door. Swinging it open, I just looked at him.

"Damn, fam. Why aren't you dressed? We heading to the church in about forty-five minutes to an hour," G said, walking into the room. He sat in the very chair that I occupied earlier.

"I can't do this shit, G. I can't do it man," I said, sitting down placing my head in my hands.

"You can and you will. That's what I'm here for, bro. Where you are weak, I'm strong. When you fall, I'll always be here to pick you back up. You are my muthafuckin' brother and I'm not gonna leave yo' side, my nigga. So, come on, man. Go get ya ass in the shower."

G was my nigga if it didn't get no bigga. We ride together on everythng and I was glad he was riding with me. I got up and gathered everything I would need to get in the shower.

Turning to face G, I said, "Thanks, fam, for being there for me through this. I appreciate you more than you ever know, my nigga." G nodded his head and I walked into the bathroom.

When I came out, G wasn't sitting in the chair anymore. I felt refreshed and somewhat ready, but I was sharper than a muthafucka. I had on a black Giorgio Armani suit with a black shirt, a blue tie which was Malikhi's favorite color and two-toned black Armani dressed shoes. I was ready to go at that moment. I don't know where the burst of confidence came from, but I was ready.

I walked out into the living room and my heart swelled. There was a room full of muthafuckas sitting patiently waiting on me. All my niggas were dressed to the nines looking just like me. Nova, Monica, and Jade were amongst them. My family showed up for me. That alone made me feel good inside.

"You ready, baby?" Jade asked, walking towards me.

"Thanks for coming, Jade. I appreciate it," I said, kissing her lips.

Jade and I had been rockin' hard until the shit happened last week, but she let me grieve without all that shit talking females do. She would call and I ignored her, but that didn't stop her from sending a text letting me know she was thinking about a nigga. That's the type of woman I need in my life. I'm gonna show her just how much real soon.

We all piled up in the funeral cars that came to pick us up. There wasn't much talking, but I guess that was just what the moment called for. Pulling up to the church, many people were already there. I had to take a deep breath to prepare myself for this shit. The last time I took this walk was when I was eighteen years old and that was for my mama.

"You alright, bro?" G asked, putting his hand on my shoulder.

"Yeah, I'm good, man. Let's do this," I said, as I pulled my shades out of my breast pocket. I opened the door and we piled out.

My feet felt like I had cement blocks on as shoes, until someone grabbed my hand. I looked over and it was Jade. I felt a sense of calm at that point and I knew I was going to get through this. One of the ushers handed me an obituary. When I looked at the picture of Malikhi on the front, that made this shit real. I didn't want to believe that he was gone. I watched him come into the world August 21, 2000, and now I'm burying him October 23, 2017. Damn, this wasn't what I had in mind for my lil' cuz, but these streets ain't shit.

We all walked in as a family with everyone else walking in behind us. Lovely was on my right and Jade was on my left. I kept my eyes on the floor the closer I got to the front of the church. I was doing just fine until Lovely buckled and started screaming.

"Lord, noooooo! Nooo! No! No!"

Me and G grabbed her right before she fainted. We carried her to the section that was reserved for the family and someone brought wet napkins and applied them to her face. I had to make sure she was ok. She started to come to, then started crying all over again. I gave her some water to drink and hugged her tightly.

Looking up, I saw all my niggas at the casket.

"You wanna go up, Love," I asked, referring to the viewing of my cousin's body.

"No, I'm not ready, Scony," she said, crying into my chest.

"You have to go up before they close it, Love. I told them once they close it, I don't want it to be opened again."

"I will, I will," she sobbed.

"I'll be right back," I told her.

I got up and made my way to the casket. My cousin looked like he was sleeping. He had on the same get up as the rest of us. We matched his fly today. G came over and wrapped his arm around my shoulder.

"He's good now, fam. These niggas about to feel it."

"You already know, man," I said, leaning down kissing my cousin on his forehead.

I turned around to go sit down and Lovely was right behind me. I grabbed her and and brought her forward. She started rubbing his face, saying 'my baby' over and over. She started crying and I knew that she was about to break. I held her tightly by the shoulders and she started patting his chest.

"Wake up, Khi! Please wake up, baby! Khi, wake up!"

She was yelling and crying. I tried to lead her away, but she wouldn't budge. I didn't want her to get out of hand, so I picked her up and told them to close it up.

"No! He won't be able to breathe! Please don't close it, please! He's gonna wake up! He's gonna wake up!" she yelled. There wasn't a dry eye in the church during Lovely's meltdown, even my own.

By the time I got her outside, she passed out again, but this time I didn't see her chest moving. G followed me out and saw me lay her down before I started CPR.

"Call an ambulance, bro! She's not breathing!" I yelled.

G did what I asked and after three minutes, I got her back. The ambulance arrived, and the EMTs put her on the stretcher. Putting an oxygen mask on her face, they loaded her into the back of the ambulance. I had my aunt ride with her to the hospital, so I could stay for the rest of the service. I'll check on her as soon as everything was over.

Chapter 32
G

My lil' homie went out in style. I wouldn't have wanted it any other way. We are going to be there for Lovely so she didn't backslide. I knew she was hurting, but we got her. We left the cemetery and now we were on our way to the hospital to check on Lovely.

When we got there, Aunt Sarah was walking out with Lovely. "What did they say, auntie?" Scony asked.

"She went into temporary shock and forgot to breathe the doctor explained. She hasn't said a word yet. And she seems like she's just here, with no life in her. I'm gonna take her back to the rehab center right now. I'll explain to the staff what happened when I get there," she said, looking at Lovely.

"Ok, bet," I said, walking them to the car. Lovely got in and immediately closed her eyes.

"Lovely, we gon' get through this, ok? Don't shut me out. Call me if you need anything. I'll be by to see you on your visiting day," Scony said, kissing her forehead.

She only nodded her head yes. He tapped on the hood of the car and stepped back.

"It's time to trade these suits in for something a little more durable. This city is about to hear my roar, my nigga," he said, walking back to my ride.

The silence in the car was deafening. Scony was in deep thought. I grabbed my phone and called my future.

When she answered, she sounded like she was sleeping. The ladies didn't go to the cemetery with us because I didn't know if anything was going to pop off, so I sent them home.

"Hey, babe. Did I wake you?" I asked.

"Nah, I was watching tv with Lady," she said, yawning.

Nova hadn't said much about finding a place since she first mentioned it over a week ago. Shit, I wasn't trying to bring it back up either. I enjoyed waking up to her in my bed. That's the best feeling a nigga done had in a long ass time.

"Nova, Lady better not be in the bed, ma. Her ass has gotten use to that shit. Now when I come home, I have to force her out."

"Baby, stop with all that. This is my baby. She won't leave my side. She keeps me company while you're away, so leave her be, please," she chuckled.

"Anyway, I was calling to let you know that I'm on my way. Did you cook?"

We didn't go to the repast, so a nigga was hungry as fuck and my baby can throw down in the kitchen.

"I knew you would be, so yeah. I cooked some spaghetti, fried some chicken, and catfish with garlic bread. Do you want me to fix a plate for you?" she asked.

"Nah, wait a while. I'll be there in about twenty minutes. I'm about to drop Scony off first."

"Shid, no the fuck you ain't, nigga! Aye, sis, *we* on our way."

My baby was laughing hard as hell. "Alright, there's enough for you, too, Scony. I'll see you when you get here, baby," she said, hanging up.

She always hung up fast and shit. I wanted to tell her I loved her, but she didn't give a nigga a chance. Then when we are laid up under each other, the words won't come out. I didn't know what the fuck was wrong with my ass, but I knew I wasn't letting her pretty ass go though.

"Man, what the fuck yo' ass over there smiling about? I told you when we first saw her ass she was gonna have you wide open. Nigga done went and fell in love and shit," Scony laughed, pulling out a blunt.

"Nigga, you said that shit like I'm ashamed or some shit. Nope! I'll wear this shit with pride. She's a keeper, my nigga."

"Yeah, I know, cream puff ass muthafucka!"

That nigga punched me in the shoulder, laughing 'til tears started falling down his face, but his laughter turned into sobs. I didn't say shit. I just kept driving. I already knew what time it was. All we had to do was gear up.

It was close to six o'clock in the evening, and it was going down in a couple of hours. By the time I pulled up to my crib, Scony had gotten himself together.

"I'm sorry about that man—" he started to say before I cut him off. +6

"You ain't never gotta apologize for crying, my nigga. We have been through too much shit for me to judge yo' ass about anything. You have a right to cry as much as you want to," I said, pulling in the garage.

"I miss that lil' nigga, G. Malikhi was more like my son than my cousin you know. This shit is fucked up, man," he said, shaking his head.

Seeing him laying there in that casket will be in my head for a long time. Everytime I close my eyes, that's the first image I see.

"I know, man, this shit ain't easy for me either. But Khi won't be forgotten, know that. He will forever live in our hearts. Let's go in here and eat so we can head out. We got a couple potatoes to peel around this bitch." We both laughed getting out the car.

Walking in the kitchen, Nova was standing at the stove making a hefty plate of food. My mouth started watering and it smelled good. I slid up behind her and wrapped my arms around her waist. After kissing her neck and then her cheek, I palmed her ass.

"Baby, ummmm, stop!" she said sternly.

I walked to to the table with my lips poked out.

"Nigga, you need to stop acting like a spoiled as kid," Scony said, laughing heartily.

"Nigga, shut yo' cockblockin ass up! You the reason she is acting like that!" I spat, cutting my eyes at his ass.

Nova placed our plates in front of us and I silently blessed our food and dove in.

"Damn, nigga, this shit is good as hell. You wanna share sis two days out of the week? I can get used to this."

This nigga was shoving food in his mouth like he didn't just say that bullshit.

"Nigga, I love ya, but I'll kill yo' ass if you say some mo' shit like that. Ain't no sharing in this muthafucka, punk ass nigga."

"Yeah, yo' ass in love," he said, laughing.

I couldn't even deny that shit, so I kept eating. I looked over at Nova and she just stood there with a smile on her face.

"Baby, come sit down for a minute. I want to talk to you about something."

"What's going on, baby?" she asked, sitting down.

I put my fork down and rubbed my hand down my face. "What I'm about to tell you may make you feel some kind of way, but I gotta say it. I found out what happened at the club the night you were shot. I got confirmatiom that your ex, Kelvin, shot you, baby, and Ziva set it up."

Nova looked at me long and hard before responding.

"Ziva wouldn't do nothing like that, Grant. She is my friend. We been rockin' since we were in grammar school, baby. I can't believe what you're saying right now," she said, now standing up.

"Baby, sit down, please. I know you don't want to believe what I'm saying, but she ain't ya friend. When was the last time you heard from her? When was the last time you *saw* her?

She didn't even come to the hospital to be by your side when you got shot. Nova, she's fuckin' that nigga! And ain't no telling how long it's been going on."

She was sitting there letting the shit I said marinate in her mind, since I didn't give her a chance to come up with another excuse.

"The day you came home from the hospital, her and Mo had words. It wasn't even thirty minutes later and yo' crib got shot up. Everybody heard about that shit Nova, but where the fuck was your *friend*? No muthafuckin' where to be found. I'm here to let you know that her days are numbered, baby. She helped that nigga run up in my shit and stole from me! But that's not why I'm mad. I'm seeing red right now because Malikhi lost his life behind that shit and you could have lost yours, too. So, when I catch up with her funky ass, she is gonna take her last muthafuckin' breath."

I waited for her to say something, but she didn't. Instead she got up and grabbed her phone. She dialed out five times without connecting with anyone. She looked at me and asked, "Are you sure about this, baby?"

"I'm positive. I wouldn't bring shit to you without doing my homework first. I'm heading out in a few to paint the streets red. I won't go into details, but just know the goon in me has surfaced," I said, getting up to put my plate in the sink.

"Sis, I wouldn't let him tell you this shit if it wasn't true. Everybody involved is gonna rest for eternity. We held off telling you because there was so much shit going on at the time. And I wanted to wait until I buried my lil' cousin. But the wait is over, sis. We can't sit around and let these niggas think we are some bitch made niggas," Scony said very calmly.

"Call Monica and Jade to come over for the night. I don't want you alone."

Meesha

I kissed her on her cheek and went to gear up.

Chapter 33
Nova

The shit that Grant told me had me thinking a little too hard. It's hard to believe that Ziva would try to hurt me. I had to get some insight on this from my girls, so I picked up my phone up and dialed them on three-way.

"Heyyyy, boo!" Mo sang into the phone.

"Hold on. Let me get Jade on the line," I said, before adding her to the call.

"Hey, Nova, what's up?" Jade asked.

"Mo is on the line, as well, Jade but I need y'all to come to G's house. I'm texting the address to both of ya'll now, I have something to talk to y'all about. But I have a question. Have y'all heard from Z at all?"

"Nova, fuck Ziva! That bitch ain't been seen since we left the fuckin' club. She is dead to me. If she was on fire, I wouldn't piss on that hoe. She did you dirty, Nova. Fuck Ziva!" Mo was mad and she don't get mad like that for nothing. I know she had some things to get off her chest.

"Nah, sis, I haven't heard from her at all, but I'm on my way right now," Jade said, hanging up.

"Nova, I hope you haven't talked to that bitch and forgiven her for her absence. I hope that's not the case. I'll see you in a few."

Monica ended the call and I went to get dressed.

***

Monica and Jade was sitting in the family room waiting for me to bring the food and drinks back. I was wondering what their take on this situation was going to be. With G telling me the shit he did and Monica going off in the manner she did, I had to believe that Ziva hated me. That was a hard pill to swallow.

I tried calling her plenty of times and my calls went unanswered. It had been almost two months since I'd seen her, so that alone justified itself, no questions asked. But we'd been through so much shit together and it was hard to block that out. Twenty plus years of friendship couldn't deteriorate for no reason at all, I didn't understand any of this. If she didn't like me, why did she constantly want to be around me? It was always 'best friend this', or 'best friend that'. I had so many questions and I knew the only person that would be able to give me the answers was Ziva.

Walking into the room, I sat the tray on the table and sat down.

"What is it that you want to talk to us about, sis?" Jade asked.

"Well, G came in today and laid some shit on me that I can't fathom. He said that Ziva had something to do with me getting shot at the club and she was the reason my house got shot up. He also told me about his trap getting robbed and Scony's cousin getting killed. Ziva and Kelvin had everything to do with that, as well. But when he told me that Kelvin and Ziva was fuckin' around, I couldn't believe that at all."

"I knew it, bitch! That man opened your eyes to the shit I been telling you on the regular. That hoe wasn't throwing shade your way for nothing all these years. That bitch been fuckin' his bum ass from the beginning. I told you to leave that hatin' ass bitch alone a long time ago! But nooooo, that's your *friend*." Mo wasn't gonna let me get a word in, so I didn't even try to say anything.

"That bitch was using you! All you were to her was a damn bank! Every time her ass fell short, she came to you! When she couldn't come up with her tuition in school, she came to you! Shid, if one didn't know, you were the mammy! Hell yeah, I'm pissed off because you gave her too much mutha-fuckin' credit. She wasn't even close to being loyal. But I can tell you one thing, that bitch gettin' that ass tapped on my mama!" Monica walked out the room and slammed a door. I didn't know what part of the house she was in, all I knew was that she was pissed.

Jade sat there not saying anything. She bit her bottom lip, shaking her head.

"Sis, Mo is mad because what she is saying is true. Ziva has been on bullshit since I've known her. I've seen how she looked at you. There was so much hate in her eyes whenever she she was around. We tried to tell you many times, but you were blind to the fact. I'm not blaming you for it, but all the signs were there, you just weren't trying to see them. Ziva violated, boo. She's done! We ain't fuckin' with her no mo'. You would be one dumb female to forgive her ass after this shit. You could have died twice and that bitch showed no remorse. That bitch named Karma is a beast and she's gonna meet her real soon," she yelled, sitting back on the couch.

Even my girls knew Ziva was foul. Yeah, this friendship is over. Shit, the way I got read over her ass and with the facts alone, it's been over.

***

I went downstairs to the basement and got my baby, Lady, and let her come upstairs. I opened the patio door so she could go out and take care of her business. I turned around and both of my girls were standing there.

"That's a beautiful dog. I've heard about Miss Lady, but I haven't seen her until now," Jade said, looking out at Lady.

"Yeah, she is a sweetie. I love her and her daddy. Yeah, I said it, I love that man. He has been everything through this ordeal. I've finally found real love."

I was smiling and my heart was warm. It's been so long since I've felt this and I didn't want it to ever end.

"Awwww, my sissy is in love. When is the wedding?" Monica joked.

"It's too soon for all that now. You are taking it a little too far, Mo."

Shaking my head, I opened the sliding door and called for Lady to come in. Running at full speed, she climbed the stairs and jumped right in my arms licking my face.

"Down, girl," I said, falling backwards with Lady on top of me. "Off, Lady! You're heavy!"

She got up and walked around to sniff Jae and Mo.

"Sit, Lady. Good girl"

"Y'all, I want to get out of this house. How about we hit the mall and do some shopping therapy?" I asked, leading Lady back to the basement and making sure she was good with food and water.

"I'm down with that. Let's go," Mo said, running for her purse.

We decided to hit Woodfield Mall in Schaumburg. The malls in the city were ghetto as hell, so we didn't even waste our time going to any of them. As we cruised on the expressway, we were singing along with the music when a car slammed on their brakes in front of me. I had to swerve onto the shoulder to avoid a collision. I paused for a minute to catch my breath. I was shaking badly, that shit scared the fuck out of me. I hated when people stopped suddenly for no reason. I'm glad I was paying attention, because the outcome could have been detrimental for all of us.

"Why the hell did that stupid muthafucka do that shit! There wasn't even anything in front of that damn car! I can't stand non-driving people. If you are scared to drive on the expressway, take the damn street!" Mo was livid.

"Are you good, Nova? I can drive if you want me to, boo."

"No, I'm okay. I'll just sit her for a couple minutes to calm my nerves."

A few minutes later, I was signaling to get back on the expressway. I drove carefully to our destination. When we exited the car, Mo started walking full speed in the opposite direction of the mall. I ran after her asking her what was wrong.

"Mo, what the hell is going on? Slow your ass down and talk to me!" I was skipping to keep up with this chic.

"Oh, hell yeah. We talked that bitch up. Now we can see what the fuck she gotta say," Jade said, walking just as fast as Mo.

I finally saw what the excitement was about. Ziva was walking toward us with another female. They were laughing and giggling like they were best of friends and shit. When we got close to them, I was the first to speak.

"What up, Z? Long time, no see, boo. I've been hittin' your line and ain't got shit back. What's up with that?"

"I don't owe you no explanation, Nova. Ask ya muthafuckin' friend why I ain't been around. If she hadn't been talking slick on the phone, I wouldn't have stayed away. But I don't fuck wit' her, so in turn I stopped fuckin' with you. I'm sorry I wasn't there when you went through your little shit, but hey friends come and go," she said, rolling her eyes as she tried to walk around me. I stepped in front of her and she stopped in her tracks.

"My little shit? That's what you call me almost getting my brains splattered all over that club, Z? After all the shit I did for you, that's how you feel, bitch?"

The shit that just came out her mouth pissed me off to the highest point of pisstivity. That was mad disrespectful. Before I knew it, I was on her ass faster than lightening. I grabbed her by that fake ass weave she had in her head and gave her the business. She must've forgot that I was crucial with these hands.

I was sweeping her ass across that parking lot, then I heard Mo say, "Bitch, if you think about it, I'm gonna fuck you up. It's one on one bitch. Ain't no jumping, but you can try that shit and get that ass tapped right along side this hoe." Ziva fell and I stomped that bitch ears together and pulled her back to her feet. As I was punching her in the face, I was screaming with every hit. Everything that everybody said to me came flooding back in my mind full force.

"Bitch, you did me dirty as hell! You didn't think I was gonna find out you was fucking that bum ass nigga? Your ass been jealous of me from day one, but now I'm showing your ass to never cross the bitch that was down for ya stupid ass!"

The bitch fell and tried to take me down with her, but I wasn't going. I braced myself and kicked that bitch square in her face. I bloodied that bitch, now I was done.

"Come on, y'all. These white people done called the muthafuckin' police, and it ain't gonna take them thirty minutes to get here," Mo said.

I looked back and the bitch she was with was leading her back to the car they had just got out of.

Chapter 34
G

The whole crew met up at the Dungeon, ready to go after this nigga Sergio. But first, I wanted to put some heat under that nigga Kelvin's ass.

"Listen up. I asked y'all to meet me here because we're about to go at this nigga Sergio full force. Him and that nigga Kelvin and whoever else was with them committed the ultimate violation. Now that Khi is resting peacefully, it's time to get in these streets and pop theses thangs like we in Baghdad."

I was standing in the middle of all my soldiers. We hadn't had to gear up for war in years. These niggas out here knew better, but it took a group of dumb muthafuckas to come at a whole tribe of killas. I tried to keep this shit on the legit side and stay out of these streets, but when a muthafucka come for mine, they weren't looking to breathe again. I hoped they made peace with the man upstairs because that's where I was sending them. It was time to remind these niggas who they fuckin' with."

I had a couple of my niggas watching Sergio's spot, seeing what the fuck his bitch ass was about. Obviously, he was just hood rich off my shit. Without it, he was trash. Even if the nigga got up on his own, he would fall flat on his face. The nigga was a flash box, wasting money on bullshit. But it didn't matter, he had time for one last turn up before I silenced his ass forever.

"I want to go on that block busting. No mask, no cars. Just straight gunplay. Light that bitch up and hit every nigga out there I don't give a fuck who it is. That block about to be hot tonight, baby. Y'all done brought the Goon Squad out of retirement, muthafuckas!"

"Gooooon Squaaaaaadd!" filled the Dungeon on one accord. "Let's ride."

We rolled to the west side deep, we parked in the alley
right off Homan. Half of us went to the north end of Christiana
Avenue and the rest went to the south end of the street. The
plan was to attack these niggas from all angles. We made our
way down the street, and pulled out all kinds artillery.

Running up on them niggas was easy. None of them niggas were on alert. We started blasting, lighting the block up
like the Fourth of July. Bodies was falling like dominos
around that bitch. Niggas tried to run and got sprayed, getting
hit wherever the bullets pierced. This one little nigga ran up
like he was king of the muthafuckin' hood with his glock
raised. I shot that nigga right between his fuckin' eyes.

I saw that nigga Sergio trying to crawl to his crib. Me and
Scony peeped that shit at the same time. We ran towards that
muthafucka and shot his ass four times more then they shot
Malikhi. The air was filled with gunpowder smoke and niggas
was laid out everywhere. Don't fuck with the Goon Squad,
muthafuckas. We left the whole muthafuckin' block covered
in blood, call it a fuckin' ghetto massacre, bitch!

***

The shit that went down on Christiana was just the beginning of what the fuck was to come. That muthafucka named
Kelvin was still hiding out, but the Goons were out baby. It
was time to make that nigga come looking for me. He
wouldn't come face the music like a man, so I'll have to force
him out like cheese to a rat.

Me, Scony, Antonio and Quan were the ones taking care
of this one. It was ten o'clock at night and we were sitting
outside this nigga mama's house. I didn't usually fuck around
with a muthafucka's family, but this nigga made me go against

what I believed in, everybody was fair game at that point. I wanted that nigga's head.

"G, are you sure you wanna do this shit, man?" Quan asked me.

"Hell yeah, my nigga. Ain't no turning back. Quan and Tonio, y'all go to the back, me and Scony got the front. Kick that bitch in as soon as y'all hear the front door bust open. Y'all got it?" I asked, looking around the car.

"We got it. Let's get it, my nigga," Tonio said, getting out the car.

The lights were on inside the house, so somebody was up in that bitch. We got in place at front the door and I didn't hesitate to kick that bitch off the hinges. We stormed in, with guns drawn. A nigga ran out the kitchen and got blasted. The back door came tumbling down and another muthafucka came running up the stairs from the basement. Antonio shot that nigga square in the chest and it exited through his back. Blood splattered on the wall behind him, leaving a trail as he fell.

I ran upstairs and to the bedroom on the left. I guess that was his mom's laying in the bed not moving. I walked up to her ass and slit her throat. I heard some shit from a room down the hall. I raced toward that room and heard what I thought was a window opening. When I got to the room, nobody was there, but I looked out the window and saw a nigga hauling ass across the backyard next door.

"Yo, out back! Somebody got out!" I yelled, running down the stairs. By the time I got downstairs, Quan was coming back in.

"That nigga got away, G, but we checked the rest of the house and it's clear. Let's get the fuck outta here, nigga," Quan said.

We left that muthafucka the same way we came in, out the front door. Come find me, nigga. You take one of mine, I wipe out all yours.

Chapter 35
Nova

It's been a week since I beat the fuck out of Ziva. G and his crew went on a killing spree to avenge Malikhi's death. He basically had me in this house under lock and key. I need to get out of this house. I've been sick a lot lately and I don't know what the hell is going on. Come to think of it, my cycle is late like a muthafucka. I got to get to the store quickly. I can't possibly be pregnant. I was hoping it was just the stress from everything that had been going on.

I hurried up and threw on my shoes and grabbed my keys. I jumped in my car and drove to the Walgreens down the street. I hopped out and went straight to the feminine hygiene aisle and snatched five different tests off the shelf. Walking to the counter, I paid for the items and left. I decided I didn't want to be home by myself taking these tests, so I called Mo.

"Yo, Nova, what's up?"

"Where are you, Mo? Please tell me you're home," I said with panic in my voice.

"Yes, I'm at home, sis. What's wrong?" she asked, getting scared herself.

"Nothing's wrong, but I'll explain it when I get there, ok?"

"Alright, hurry up. I'll be here waiting. Wait! Do I need to call Jade, too?" she asked.

"Yeah, you may as well. I'll be there in a minute," I said, hanging up.

I guess this would be a good time to call G and let him know where I'll be. I dialed his number and he answered on the first ring.

"What's up, my future? What you doing?"

"I'm on my way to Monica's house, so I knew I had to call to let you know."

"Baby, why didn't you call me and let me know that you wanted to go out? I would have stopped what I was doing and took you over there myself. I don't want you out like that when these muthafuckas are still out here in these streets."

He was mad because he was yelling. I started crying on cue. "Where the fuck did that come from?" I asked myself. I have never cried that easy and over something so stupid at that.

"Why are you crying, Nova? I'm just concerned about you right now. I don't know what I would do if something happened to you. Just call me when you make it to Monica's, ok?"

"Ok, I will. I love you, Grant Davenport."

"I love you more, Nova Lacour," he said, disconnecting the call.

I pulled up to Monica's house and got out of the car, not forgetting to grab the bag with the tests in it. Before I could knock on the door, it was snatched opened.

"Nova, what's wrong, and why are you crying?" she asked, hugging me.

"G yelled at me because I left the house to come over here. He said I should've called him. He's mad at me, Mo," I said, crying uncontrollably.

Mo let me go, looked me in my face and started smiling.

"Sis, are you pregnant, because your ass is overly sensitive right now?"

"I don't know. That's why I came over here. I've been sick a lot these past couple of days and my cycle is late. I went to Walgreens and bought some tests." I said, holding up the bag and Monica started laughing.

"Come on you, big baby. Let's see what the hell is going on."

Just when we were about to go to the back room, someone knocked on the door. Monica went to answer it, and it was Jae.

"What's the damn emergency? Nova, what's wrong?" she asked, throwing her purse on the table by the door.

"This crybaby is pregnant as hell, that's what's wrong." Monica said, laughing.

"Don't say that, Monica! I haven't even taken the tests yet!" I started crying all over again.

"Yeah, you're pregnant. Let's go," Jae said.

We went to the bathroom and these two fools stood there like they were gonna watch.

"Would you guys get out and closed the door, please? I have never pissed in front of y'all and I'm not about to start now."

I pushed them out of the door and opened all five tests. I relieved my bladder, catching enough in the cup that was provided in one of the boxes. I dipped all five tests and laid them on the counter. I wiped myself, flushed the toilet and washed my hands. This was the longest two minutes of my life. After a while, Monica busted through the door with Jade following behind her.

"What did it say, sis?" Monica asked.

"I don't know. I'm scared to look. Would you look for me?"

"I'll look, shit. I already know what the results are without looking anyway," Jae said, walking over to the counter.

She didn't have to say anything at all, the big smile on her face told it all.

"You are pregnant five times according to these tests right here," she screamed, jumping up and down. "I'm gonna be an auntie," she sang, dancing around.

"Congratulations, brat!" Monica hugged me so tight, but I was numb. I didn't know what to say.

"What will G say? Does he even want to be a daddy? Will he leave me?" I asked these questions without taking a breath. I was nervous and scared shitless.

"Stop talking crazy, that man loves you, sis. He will be so happy. The question is when are you gonna tell him?" Mo asked with a raised eyebrow.

"I'm gonna make it a surprise, turn it into a game. I'm going to stop at Michaels and pick up some cute stuff. I'll do a scavenger hunt type of thing, make him look for clues," I said, collecting the tests putting them back in the bag.

"That sounds like fun! You have to make sure you are recording it. I want to see his reaction," Jade said.

"I can go to the store with you, Nova." Mo said grabbing her purse and keys.

"I won't be in there long. I just have a few things to get out of there. Plus, it's on the way home and that would be taking you out of your way. I'm good, Mo." She looked at me like she wanted to say something else, but didn't.

"I'm about to go so I can get everything set up at the house. I'll call ya'll when I get there and thank y'all so much for always being there. I love y'all."

"We love you, too," both said. We hugged and I left out the door.

I called G when I was backing out of Mo's driveway. He picked up instantly.

"Hey, baby, are you on your way home?" he asked.

"Yes, that's why I was calling. I will call you as soon as I step foot in the house.

"Okay, love. Be safe and I love you.

"Always and I love you, too."

I disconnected the call and my music app started playing instantly. I headed to Micheals to get what I needed to surprise my big baby with the news of our little baby.

Chapter 36
Kelvin

These niggas had lost their muthafuckin' minds. They went through my man Sergio's spot and killed everybody on the block including him. When I heard that shit, I broke down because that was my nigga. I felt guilty for getting him mixed up in my shit. We got paid, but that didn't mean shit when you were deader than a doorknob. When I went on Christiana, the blood was still on the pavement.

Many people said that the Goon Squad did it. I hadn't heard that name in years, so I knew they were in killa mode. If they got Sergio, it wouldn't be long before they came after me. I had been ducked off for a long while. It was a good thing that Z was the only one that knew where I laid my head. I started parking my car in the garage of my complex just in case them niggas found out where I lived. I wasn't a stupid nigga by far.

Speaking of Ziva, she called me and told me how Nova and her croonies jumped on her. She had a broken eye socket and a bunch of bumps and bruises. They fucked shorty up pretty bad. I felt sorry for her, so I took care of her until she was better.

The worst part of it all was the fact that them niggas killed my mama! I was in the house that night along with my brothers when them niggas kicked the door in. I heard the gunshots and started looking for a way out. I finally got to the window and jumped out. I cried all the way to my crib because my mama was all I had left.

But they fucked with the wrong muthafucka. Yeah, I was the reason Scony's cousin was killed and I was the one that broke Nova's jaw and shot her ass, but she deserved all that shit. And I'll do it all over again. I had plans to slit her mutha-fuckin throat the same way them muthafuckas did my mama!

My phone rang and it was Ziva. I hadn't talked to her or Avah since that shit went down a week ago. I pushed the phone icon and answered. "What's up, baby girl? How are you doing?

"I'm good. I was at Home Depot getting new blinds and when I came out, guess who I saw coming out of Michaels?" she asked with excitement.

"Who did you see, Z? Stop bullshitting and just tell me, man." She pissed me off when she stalled and shit.

"I saw Nova. She is the reason everything is going on, baby. I refuse to let her live a lavish life while these niggas are looking for you. She had to pay for the shit she's been putting you through. I hit her ass over her head with a bat when she was bending over in her car. I guess she forgot that she can be touched. Her man should've warned her about checking her surroundings." Ziva was excited as hell that she just assaulted this woman.

"Ziva, where is Nova now? What did you do with her?" I was curious to know what her plans were or if she was stupid enough to do it and leave her there.

"I put the bitch in my trunk. We can kill her ass now, Kelvin. Plus, she can tell us where that nigga G is at." She waited to hear what I had to say.

She had a point, I can make this bitch tell me everything she knows or she will fuckin' die.

"Bring that bitch to me, Z. You did good, baby. I'll be waiting when you get here."

When Ziva pulled up, I was already outside. I jumped in the car and told her to drive. I couldn't keep anyone hostage in a fuckin' apartment. My mama has a ranch house in Itasca. It sat on about four acres of land and no neighbors for about two miles. It was the perfect stash spot, that is now mine. Nobody would find her ass out there.

We drove for about thirty-five minutes then pulled up to the house. I had Z pop the trunk and I picked Nova up and carried her up the stairs. I unlocked the door and went in. The house was fully furnished and there was a basement. That was where she would be spending her time until I decided to kill her ass. She was still out cold, but I knew she as alive because her chest was moving up and down. I placed her on the bed and found some duct tape in a dresser drawer. I bounded her arms and legs to the bedpost.

At that moment, there was a noise that sounded like a cellphone coming from somewhere near Nova. I walked over to her and searched her pockets, 'My baby' was displayed on the screen. That shit made me mad, so I didn't answer the call. It rang several more times and I still didn't answer.

Nova started moving around, moaning like she was in pain. She blinked several times until her vision focused. She stared straight at me with a horrid expression on her face.

"Hello, beautiful. Did you miss me?"

"What did you do, Kelvin? Let me go! Yo' ass is crazy. You do know this is kidnapping, right?" she yelled as she started crying.

"Don't cry now, baby. You are where you belong. You have always belonged right here with me. I still love you, Nova."

"You don't love me. You tried to kill me, Kelvin! I don't have any love for you anymore. Just let me go!" she cried.

"You ain't going no damn where, bitch. You're gonna stay right here with me, my love."

At that moment, the basement door opened and Ziva came down stairs smiling.

"Hey, bestie. How are you feeling? Is that bitch Karma treating you right?" Ziva let out a laugh that sent chills through my body. This bitch was crazy.

"You bitch! I knew you wasn't shit! That's why I beat yo' muthafuckin' ass! If he let me up, I'm gonna fuck you up again, believe that!" Nova was mad talking big shit and she was restrained to the bed.

"Bitch, I can kill your ass now if I wanted to. What can you do about it?"

"Have y'all fun now because once my man finds out where I am, you two muthafuckas are gonna die. But if y'all cut this tape off my muthafuckin hands, I'll do it myself, bitch ass niggas!"

I had never heard her talk like that when she had control, but now she was defenseless and talking like a savage. Ziva must've hit her ass too hard or something. She didn't hit her with enough force to break skin, but she did enough damage to bring out another side of her.

At that point, her phone rang again and it was that nigga again. I answered that time and put it on speaker.

"What up, G?"

"Who the fuck is this and where is Nova?" he screamed into the phone.

"This is Kelvin, bitch ass nigga. I heard you've been looking for me, but since you couldn't find me you took my mama from me. That was the wrong move to make, nigga. But I took our bitch back. An eye for an eye, my nigga. Now let the games begin, muthafucka." I laughed and hung up on that nigga.

This muthafucka was going to give me what I wanted or I was going to kill this bitch. There was a time I would have done anything for Nova's ass, but the bitch fucked up when she stopped fuckin' with me. I was going to have fun fucking the shit out of her for old times sake.

Now his ass gotta come find me to get her back, and I'll be sitting right here waiting.

G was about to find out that wasn't a goddam thing sweet over this way!

To Be Continued...
A Distinguished Thug Stole My Heart 2
Coming Soon

Stay Connected with Us!

Text **LOCKDOWN** to 22828 to stay up-to-date with new releases, sneak peaks, contests and more…

Thank you!

<u>Coming Soon from Lock Down Publications/Ca$h Presents</u>

BOW DOWN TO MY GANGSTA

By **Ca$h & Jamaica**

TORN BETWEEN TWO

By **Coffee**

BLOOD OF A BOSS **IV**

By **Askari**

BRIDE OF A HUSTLA **III**

THE FETTI GIRLS **III**

By **Destiny Skai**

WHEN A GOOD GIRL GOES BAD **II**

By **Adrienne**

LOVE & CHASIN' PAPER **II**

By **Qay Crockett**

THE HEART OF A GANGSTA **II**

By **Jerry Jackson**

LOYAL TO THE GAME **IV**

By **T.J. & Jelissa**

A DOPEBOY'S PRAYER **II**

By **Eddie "Wolf" Lee**

THE BOSS MAN'S DAUGHTERS **III**

By **Aryanna**

TRUE SAVAGE **III**

By **Chris Green**

IF LOVING YOU IS WRONG… **II**

By **Jelissa**

BLOODY COMMAS **II**

By **T.J. Edwards**

A DISTINGUISHED THUG STOLE MY HEART **II**

By **Meesha**

ADDICTIED TO THE DRAMA

By **Jamila Mathis**

<u>Available Now</u>

(CLICK TO PURCHASE)

RESTRAINING ORDER **I & II**

By **CA$H & Coffee**

LOVE KNOWS NO BOUNDARIES **I II & III**

By **Coffee**

RAISED AS A GOON I, II & III

By **Ghost**

LAY IT DOWN **I & II**

LAST OF A DYING BREED

By **Jamaica**

LOYAL TO THE GAME

LOYAL TO THE GAME II

LOYAL TO THE GAME III

By **TJ & Jelissa**

BLOODY COMMAS

By **T.J. Edwards**

IF LOVING HIM IS WRONG…

By **Jelissa**

PUSH IT TO THE LIMIT

By **Bre' Hayes**

BLOOD OF A BOSS **I II & III**

By **Askari**

THE STREETS BLEED MURDER **I, II & III**

THE HEART OF A GANGSTA

By **Jerry Jackson**

CUM FOR ME

CUM FOR ME 2

CUM FOR ME 3

An **LDP Erotica Collaboration**

BRIDE OF A HUSTLA **I & II**

THE FETTI GIRLS **I & II**

By **Destiny Skai**

WHEN A GOOD GIRL GOES BAD

By **Adrienne**

A GANGSTER'S REVENGE **I II III & IV**

THE BOSS MAN'S DAUGHTERS

THE BOSS MAN'S DAUGHTERS II

A SAVAGE LOVE **I & II**

Meesha

BAE BELONGS TO ME

A HUSTLER'S DECEIT I, II

By **Aryanna**

A KINGPIN'S AMBITON

A KINGPIN'S AMBITION **II**

I MURDER FOR THE DOUGH

By **Ambitious**

TRUE SAVAGE

TRUE SAVAGE II

By **Chris Green**

A DOPEBOY'S PRAYER

By **Eddie "Wolf" Lee**

WHAT ABOUT US **I & II**

NEVER LOVE AGAIN

THUG ADDICTION

By **Kim Kaye**

THE KING CARTEL **I, II & III**

By **Frank Gresham**

THESE NIGGAS AIN'T LOYAL **I, II & III**

By **Nikki Tee**

GANGSTA SHYT **I II &III**

By **CATO**

THE ULTIMATE BETRAYAL

By **Phoenix**

BOSS'N UP **I & II**

By **Royal Nicole**

I LOVE YOU TO DEATH

By Destiny J

I RIDE FOR MY HITTA

I STILL RIDE FOR MY HITTA

By **Misty Holt**

LOVE & CHASIN' PAPER

By **Qay Crockett**

TO DIE IN VAIN

By **ASAD**

<u>BOOKS BY LDP'S CEO, CA$H</u>
(CLICK TO PURCHASE)

<u>TRUST IN NO MAN</u>

<u>TRUST IN NO MAN 2</u>

<u>TRUST IN NO MAN 3</u>

<u>BONDED BY BLOOD</u>

<u>SHORTY GOT A THUG</u>

<u>THUGS CRY</u>

<u>THUGS CRY 2</u>

<u>THUGS CRY 3</u>

<u>TRUST NO BITCH</u>

<u>TRUST NO BITCH 2</u>

<u>TRUST NO BITCH 3</u>

<u>TIL MY CASKET DROPS</u>

<u>RESTRAINING ORDER</u>

<u>RESTRAINING ORDER 2</u>

<u>IN LOVE WITH A CONVICT</u>

<u>Coming Soon</u>

BONDED BY BLOOD 2

BOW DOWN TO MY GANGSTA